FROM WATSON'S SCRAPBOOK

I do suspect that most of my readers are well aware that my dear friend Holmes is loath to display anything remotely like what other spirits might call "emotion"—but not only is this an exterior perspective, but those who know him as well as I do—oh, do let me amend that!—*I* am aware that he only does this to distance himself from anything that might, perhaps, interfere with that cold clear reason that he applies to his cases.

And yet, I am pleased to report, this singularly "emotionless" gentleman displays considerable feeling whenever *Sherlock Holmes Mystery Magazine* reaches any of its 5 issues, for when it does, my colleague and coeditor Mr Kaye, devotes all of its contents to The Great Detective! This pleases my friend immensely, for though he may prefer for us to think that he is a calculating device that must never be contaminated with affairs of the heart, rather than the mind, he freely admits that he possesses quite an healthy ego—a fact seconded by his brother Mycroft, who does not exercise such a faculty because, in his own words, "It takes far too much effort, and, of course, my younger sibling has ever so much more energy than do I!"

So here we are at our fifteenth issue, and, as Holmes's old criminal acquaintance Raffles might say, "The man really kvells at any publicity, be it positive or negative." ("Kvell," I might add, is an expression employed by those of the Hebraic persuasion to denote great joy.)

Thus, this issue features pieces concerning Holmes's and my radio appearances (I thoroughly enjoyed narrating many of the latter), as well as what I found to be a fascinating article discussing the typical elements of a published case, and how they were present from the beginning.

As for the fiction in this issue, let me remark that many times in this periodical, superb renditions of my nearly unreadable notes about cases I had not got around to writing have been both deciphered and written by nine excellent authors, only of whom (Ms Carla Coupe) is missing from this lineup. The others are (alphabetically) Ms Carole Buggé, Eugene D Goodwin, J D Grimmer, Jack Grochot, Dr Bruce Kilstein, Mark Levy, Gary Lovisi, and Adam McFarlane.

Also included is one of my least familiar efforts, a brief piece I wrote for the Queen's Doll's House (details appear at the top of the story). It has been attributed to my agent Conan Doyle, but I wish to correct the record and claim it as my own, though it is hardly my most sterling of moments.

Now let me render the rest of this epistle to Mr Kaye.

—John H Watson, M D

Well, really, the good doctor has said it all for this issue. All that I am able to add here as this *post scriptum* is what our readers may expect in our upcoming sixteenth issue. In addition to two Holmesian adventures, one by Watson himself and one written from his notes by Jack Grochot, there will be a generous supply of new articles and stories, including works by "recidivists" Marc Bilgrey, Dianne Neral Ell, Steve Liskow, R. J. Lewis, and Laird Long.

—Canonically Yours,
Marvin Kaye

COMING NEXT TIME...

STORIES! ARTICLES!
SHERLOCK HOLMES & DR. WATSON!

Sherlock Holmes Mystery Magazine #16
is just a few months away...watch for it!

DEAR DOCTOR WATSON

by Dr John H. Watson

As the reading public is no doubt aware, I devote much of my time to chronicling the cases of Mr. Sherlock Holmes, the world's first consulting detective. Because of the sheer number of cases which Holmes has been involved in, recounting his adventures has become a full time endeavor for me. What my dear readers may not be aware of, is that in addition to being Holmes' biographer and often assisting him on his cases, it is also my task to respond to the many letters from the public that arrive at our Baker Street rooms daily.

Much of the mail received contains questions about Holmes and his cases and I make my best efforts to answer as many of these as time allows. What follows are some recent missives that have found their way to my desk. I publish these with the hope that they will give some insight into Sherlock Holmes both the man and the detective.

✗　　✗　　✗　　✗

Dear Dr Watson,

What is Sherlock Holmes like between cases?

—Delving in Dover

✗　　✗　　✗　　✗

Dear Delving,

The answer to your question is in a word, impossible. I have written about Holmes' violin playing, what I have not mentioned till now is, that he often plays "Row, Row, Row Your Boat" so often that one is inclined to never again want to set foot into another seagoing vessel, or simply throttle him where he stands, or perhaps both. I have at various times touched upon Holmes' pipe smoking. However, I am fairly certain I have not previously stated that there are certain days where the air at 221B is so thick with smoke that one cannot see one's own hand in front of one's face.

As a result, while attempting to walk from one room to the next, I have frequently had collisions with all manner of furniture, causing innumerable bumps, bruises, skinned knees, sprained toes, sore shins and on at least one occasion, I narrowly averted severe trauma to my medulla oblongata.

I know that I have written that Holmes has a hobby of shooting Her Royal Majesty's initials into our walls with his revolver. This in itself might be tolerable occasionally, but what I have failed to report is that he has also fired the initials of most of the rest of the Royal Family into the walls as well. As most people are aware, the Royals are a very large family filled with Dukes, Earls, Counts, Barons and numerous other lesser relations. If Holmes cannot think of a family member, he has also been known to shoot a royal servant's initials instead. Our walls now contain more lead than a mining operation in County Durham.

And then there are the scientific experiments, wherein Holmes turns our rooms into a defacto laboratory. These experiments sometimes result in explosions, and frankly, I for one, am tired of having to scrape foul-smelling toxic chemicals off my night clothes or for that matter, the ceiling. A man's home should be his castle, not a repository for the odiferous burnt and melted remains of the periodic table of elements.

And speaking of elements, I have not even touched upon Sherlock Holmes' cocaine habit. The less written about this the better. Suffice it to say that if I never again inadvertently sit down on a hypodermic needle that he's absentmindedly placed on a chair or a sofa, I believe I shall die a very happy man.

✗   ✗   ✗   ✗

Dear Dr Watson,

In your accounts of Sherlock Holmes you have upon occasion alluded to a number of untold cases. Are there others that you have not recounted?

—Literary Lady in Lancaster

✗   ✗   ✗   ✗

Dear Literary Lady,

There are many cases that I have not released to the public because they are of a sensational nature, or contain delicate matters that may pose a danger to Crown or Country. As to the others, here is a partial listing:

- Dame Prunella Bindenford's exploding tea crumpets of doom, a case much too silly to convey without giggling hysterically like a ticklish schoolgirl.

- The case of the Polite Frenchman, which the world is not yet ready to believe.

- The Horrible Haunted Haggis of Hereford Hedge, a case too filled with alliteration to easily remember, let alone repeat.

- The Odd Disappearance of the Meek File Clerk from The Department Of Weights And Measures; a case so uninteresting that the mere retelling of it has been known to induce a deep coma in all who have heard it.

✗　✗　✗　✗

Dear Dr Watson,

Was there ever a meeting between Sherlock Holmes and Professor Moriarty that you did not document?

　　　　　　　　　　　—Chester Mann in Manchester

Dear Chester,

Yes. Holmes and Moriarty once met by chance in a local pub called The Hair of the Goat. At first they exchanged heated barbs, but eventually settled down to a pint of Guinness, a friendly game of darts, and some nice mince pie. By mutual consent, they both agreed to never speak of the incident again. As I recall, through a series of intricate and elaborate ruses, Moriarty was able to stick Holmes with the bill. This may account for why Holmes has denied that this curious evening ever occurred.

✗　✗　✗　✗

Dear Dr Watson,

What case did Sherlock Holmes take the least amount of time to solve?

　　　　　　　　　　　—Surly in Surrey

✗　✗　✗　✗

Dear Surly,

The case that Holmes solved in the least amount of time was the The Mysterious Mystery of Our Missing House Keys. He found them behind an end table in under thirty seconds.

✗ ✗ ✗ ✗

Dear Dr Watson,

Has Sherlock Holmes ever been romantically interested in any women?

—Nosy in Nottingham

✗ ✗ ✗ ✗

Dear Nosy,

Yes. Holmes once had a brief fling with a hatcheck girl named Hilda at a German ratskeller near Piccadilly Square. Within a short time she left him for an overweight Zeppelin commander called Otto. Otto had a very long waxed mustache that was so sharp it punctured his aircraft and sent it crashing into a peat bog in Hampshire where the crew of fifty immediately resorted to cannibalism to stay alive; this despite the fact that the nearest town was in plain sight and well within walking distance. The whole chain of events was so disturbing to Holmes that for years afterward he would become visibly shaken at the mere mention of liverwurst or sauerbraten.

✗ ✗ ✗ ✗

Dear Dr Watson,

You have often quoted words and expressions that Sherlock Holmes uses such as "Elementary" and "The game is afoot." Are there any others that you have omitted from your writings?

—Wanting to know in Warrington

✗ ✗ ✗ ✗

Dear Wanting,

Yes. I have neglected to record for posterity Holmes' repeated use of the phrases, "Pip pip," "Talley ho," "Ta-ta, old bean," and of late, "Hubba Hubba."

Dear Dr Watson,

Why did Sherlock Homes fight Professor Moriarty on the Reichenbach Falls?

—Ignorant in Inverness

Dear Ignorant,

Because Niagara Falls was too far away.

✗

TUNING IN SHERLOCK

AN OVERVIEW OF SHERLOCK HOLMES'S LONG HISTORY ON RADIO

by John Longenbaugh

Sherlock Holmes, the world's most celebrated Consulting Detective, is older than radio itself by a few years—he first appeared in print in 1887, six years before Nikolai Tesla made the first tentative experiments in wireless communication.But Holmes was also at the very beginnings of radio drama, and he's still being heard on the air and on the internet, via both amateur and professional companies, who continue to produce their own original stories featuring the world's most celebrated sleuth.

(So for the record, that means Holmes has the longest run of any fictional character in radio—Take that, Lone Ranger!)

What is it about Holmes that fits the medium of radio so well?

Part of the appeal for radio is that when it comes to Holmes, the listener's imagination is already primed to meet the story more than halfway. The hawk-like visage and deerstalker cap, the gaslight eerily haloed above the fog-enshrouded streets, the cozy if eccentric accoutrements of 221B Baker Street—each person has a perfect picture of this late-Victorian world, and it takes little more than the recorded sound of a jingling hansom cab or a snatch of violin music to evoke it.

But the stories of Sherlock Holmes also fit themselves to radio because The Great Detective was always at his most effective in the form of the short story. With the brilliant exception of *The Hound of the Baskervilles,* Conan Doyle's hero was always happiest solving a crime in 30 pages or so, or the equivalent of a half-hour of radio listening. That's not to say that the novels haven't been successfully adapted to radio—there have been several versions over the years, including fairly recent adaptations of *The Sign of Four* and *The Valley of Fear.* But despite their quality and fidelity to Doyle's books, it is hard to imagine it taking longer than a half hour's narrative for Holmes to solve any particular crime before returning to his violin, his newspapers, and the noxious shag tobacco stored in the toe of his Persian slipper.

The first radio play featuring Sherlock Holmes aired on NBC in 1930, an adaptation of *The Speckled Band* starring the most famous stage actor to ever play Holmes, William Gillette, who came out of retirement to play the role aged 77. (He returned to play Sherlock for a Lux Radio Theatre abridged production of his famous stage version five years later.) Neither the 1930 nor 1935 recordings of Gillette still exist, but a bit of dialogue from the actor recorded to test out some sound equipment from 1936 still survives, a short exchange with Watson discussing Professor Moriarty and one with an actress playing Alice Faulkner, his love interest created by Gillette for his acclaimed stage adaptation. (Gillette, who wrote the dramatization with the blessing of Conan Doyle himself, asked if he could marry Holmes off at the end of the play. "You may marry him, murder him, do anything you like," said his creator.) Although the surviving recording is only a few minutes long, Gillette is exuberant in the role, and it's thrilling to hear the performance of one of the most critically acclaimed Holmes ever.

Immediately following this inaugural radio performance, actor Richard Gordon took over and played Holmes until 1933, when tired of the role, he left and Louis Hector took over the role of Holmes. (Hector occasionally played the role of arch-villain Professor Moriarty through the 1930s.) Leigh Lovell played Watson to Gordon's Holmes from 1930 till his death in 1935, and Gordon returned to play Sherlock for several months in 1936 with a new Watson, Henry West.

As to the few number of shows that still exist featuring Gordon and Hector, these shows aren't the best, and not just because of the poor quality of the recordings. While Lovell's Watson is an engaging performance, he's also a bit of an old duffer. And Gordon's interpretation is of a caustic and cold Holmes who's also teetering on being elderly. Hector's Holmes is in the vein of his predecessor, if not more so; at times he makes the Great Detective sound downright crotchety.

One important feature of these early shows, however, is that several of the episodes were original stories, not adaptations of Conan Doyle originals. The writer of these new adventures for

Holmes was a woman, Edith Meiser, a strikingly attractive actress/playwright who was also an avid Sherlockian. Meiser started searching for a sponsor for her proposed Sherlock Holmes series in 1927, and it took her three years to find a sponsor, G. Washington Coffee. (As a result, Watson is drinking a cup of the very un-English beverage at the start of each episode.) Meiser began writing new tales when she ran low on adaptable material in the first season, originally adapting from other Conan Doyle stories like *The Jew's Breastplate* which didn't originally feature the Great Detective. Though she wrote these adaptations without any initial permission from the Conan Doyle estate, her work was praised by Conan Doyle's children as first-rate. Meiser continued to work as the prime author on several different Sherlock Holmes series throughout the '30s and mid-'40s, including one featuring the premiere duo of the era, Basil Rathbone as Holmes and Nigel Bruce as Watson.

After their premiere in 1939's film version of *The Hound of the Baskervilles,* Rathbone and Bruce were convinced to not only produce a series of follow-up films, but to take their performances to radio too. For many older people Rathbone remains the definitive Holmes, and radio highlights his gifts of quick intelligence and classically-clipped diction. Bruce's Watson, on the other hand, is the same blustering nincompoop of the films, if not more so—his repeated failure to grasp the obvious is at best a triumph of comedy over subtlety. (Still, the radio productions often trump the films the actors made, in large part because the movies soon moved their detective to modern times for budgetary reasons.)

Eventually Rathbone grew tired of the role both on film and radio, though Bruce continued on with a new Holmes, Tom Conway, doing a serviceable Rathbone impersonation. When the show moved to the East Coast in 1947, Bruce and Conway both dropped the roles and were themselves replaced first by John Stanley as Holmes and Alfred Shirley as Watson, then two years later Ben Wright as Holmes and Eric Snowden as Watson, who saw the series to its end in 1950. With each of these later actors the definitive imprint of both Rathbone's and Bruce's performances is clearly evident, though the scripts seem to be increasingly dumbed down, as there were apparently worries from sponsors that the mysteries were too difficult for the audience to follow.

Of course, Holmes was also parodied and featured across many shows in the Golden Age of Radio, including the *Jack Benny Show* (where Jack played a Holmes in pursuit of a penthouse murderer who turns out to be King Kong), and Fred Allen on the *Texaco Star Theatre*, featuring a sketch in which Allen plays Consulting Detective Fetlock Bones. (Those who enjoy this sort of pun-filled irreverent romp might enjoy counterculture audio humorists The Firesign Theatre's 1974 album *The Giant Rat of Sumatra*, which sets their detective Hemlock Stones on the famed rodent's elusive trail.)

And there was an early attempt at gender reversal in 1946's *Meet Miss Sherlock*, in which a clever young woman named Jane Sherlock, "as smart a little gal as ever stumbled across a real live clue," solves crimes. Despite some horribly sexist lines like these from its introduction, the surviving episodes of the show are a moderately entertaining light mystery series. The template of Jane and her boyfriend Peter seems to be Gracie Allen and George Burns, with Jane concealing her native intelligence behind a scatter-brained persona.

Yet while the golden age of American radio drama was winding down, in Britain it remained a vital entertainment. And in fact the first great Holmes and Watson of British radio began two years later in 1952. (Prior to this date there had been a few adaptations of individual stories, but no ongoing series.) Carleton Hobbs and Norman Shelley, who played the roles in several series running up to 1969, performed in adaptations of Conan Doyle's originals, including excellent multi-part versions of the Holmes novels, whose length generally precluded them from adaptation in America. The series has fine audio quality and the scripts are tremendously faithful to the stories. Both actors are solid, but to my mind Hobbs is too gentle and genial as the sometimes unbearable detective, and while Shelley is an improvement over Bruce's blustering caricature, the template is the same: a well-meaning but dim sidekick who's as English, and as unimaginative, as a bulldog.

One outstanding radio incarnation around this time is a 1954-55 collection of twelve episodes featuring two great British actors, John Gielgud as Holmes and Ralph Richardson as Watson. The most successful aspect of this series is the deep and undeniable quality of mutual warmth that the two actors, life-long friends off the stage, bring to the roles. The series also benefits from a first-rate supporting cast, excellent production quality, and in the episode of *The Final Problem*, a bravura performance by Orson Welles as Professor Moriarty, the Napoleon of Crime.

(Welles himself played Holmes on radio once before, when he'd adapted the William Gillette Holmes play for an episode of his celebrated Mercury Theater program. It's fascinating hearing his portrayal, seemingly modeled on Gillette's performance, and makes one wish he'd assayed the role on film as well. For Welles buffs there's also a superb 1943 episode of *Suspense*, "The Lost Special," adapted from a Conan Doyle short story with Welles playing Herbert de Lernac, a villain of Moriarty-like brilliance.)

Various other notable radio productions include British actors Clive Merrison (as Holmes) and Michael Williams (Watson) who managed to complete a special BBC series between 1989 and 1998 of every Holmes story Conan Doyle ever wrote, and radio adaptations of stage plays by Gillette and Conan Doyle himself, produced under the title *Sherlock Holmes Theater* by Blackstone Audio Books. There's also an ambitious BBC original special from 1981 of *Sherlock Holmes Versus Dracula* that you can find for download with a bit of internet sleuthing—in fact, most of these series can be found on the internet or via such old-time radio collections as OTRCAT.

Thanks to the new popularity of the Great Detective in both the BBC's brilliant *Sherlock* series and the rather more run-of-the-mill CBS series *Elementary*, there's more interest in Holmes than ever before, and more radio drama as well. The Sherlock Holmes Society of London has a good cross-section of productions performed by different British companies, including both stories from Conan Doyle and those by modern writers. Original stories such as *The Long Man* and *The Grace Chalice* are available for free download at http://www.sherlock-holmes.org.uk/world/radio.php.

One man who's continued Sherlock's long run on radio is Seattle actor/author/radio impresario Jim French, who began his career as a writer on *Suspense* in the 1950s. French has been producing original Sherlock Holmes radio plays since 1998 as part of his Imagination Theatre. This is distributed to over 120 stations across the country, and recently published its 16th collected CD set of original adventures featuring the detective. French's series remains the only radio incarnation of Holmes officially authorized by the Conan Doyle estate. First with the late John Gilbert and now John Patrick Lowrie as Holmes, the series features the star of French's hardboiled Harry Nile series, Larry Albert, as Watson.

French's adaptations are high quality and well-acted, exhibiting the sort of seasoned production craftsmanship that once made radio shows such a delight. As far as plots, the stories tend more to the police procedural than some of the melodramatic cliff-hangers of the Rathbone/Bruce days. While this is keeping with the spirit of many of Conan Doyle's original stories, it's also not surprising from the creator of celebrated radio gumshoe Harry Nile.

There are hundreds of radio broadcasts of Sherlock Holmes, with dozens of performances, available via the internet and over the airwaves. And best of all, regardless of the actor's interpretation or the source of the plot, it's inevitably still Holmes—eccentric and infuriating, cold yet capable of surprising emotion, and always not just one step ahead of poor Watson, but of us as well.

✗

"Did you say . . . my money or my wife?"

DR. WATSON: ACTION HERO?

by Leigh Perry

Dr. John H. Watson, Dr. Sherlock Holmes's partner in crime-solving, is usually portrayed as an older gentleman in tweeds and a bowler—not exactly the archetypal action hero. That's how I pictured him myself until recent movie and TV adaptations made me change my view. It's not that he's been reimagined—the fact is, I've realized that Watson has always been a man of action.

As a mystery writer, I've long been aware that I owe a debt to Sir Arthur Conan Doyle and his influence on the genre. While I am in awe of his creation of the Great Detective, I've always considered his finest contribution to be Dr. Watson, the every-man who offers insight into the mental processes of a genius. Of course, the C. Auguste Dupin stories by Edgar Allan Poe had a similar structure—genius and sidekick—but Poe's nameless narrator was a cipher, showing none of the charm of Watson, who humanizes Holmes both for the consulting detective's clients and for the reader.

From the writer's side, I admire the character of Watson as the best method for sharing needed exposition that I've ever come across. It works like this:

1. Holmes looks at the evidence and announces his seemingly magical deductions.

2. Watson asks how he figured it out.

3. Holmes explains his reasoning.

It's so elegantly simple that it's—dare I say it—elementary. You get the best of both worlds. Doyle mystifies the reader at first, then explains the solution in a dynamic way, with dialog instead of a paragraph of static explanation.

The technique is so perfect that countless other mystery writers have followed suit. In Dorothy Sayers' Lord Peter Wimsey books, Wimsey had Inspector Parker, his man-servant Bunter, or his wife

Harriet to play the role of Watson. Rex Stout's Nero Wolfe had Archie Goodwin. Agatha Christie gave us Poirot and Hastings. Nancy Drew had two cohorts: Bess and George. S.S. Van Dine used himself as the Watson in the Philo Vance series. More recently, Martha Grimes gave Richard Jury an able assistant in Melrose Plant, and Laurie King presented Holmes himself with a new Watson via his wife, Mary Russell.

Though having a Watson around is ideal for explaining a detective's brilliant deductions, it works just as well for different kinds of exposition. Dana Cameron's Emma Fielding series features an archeologist protagonist who explains her work to her non-archeologist husband. S.J. Rozan has alternating sleuths in her Lydia Chin/Bill Smith series, and they take turns explaining their worlds to one another. Honestly, it's such a robust modus operandi that I could give examples all day long, and I'm far from the first mystery author to pay homage to Watson's role as, well, a Watson.

What I only recently came to realize is another role Watson plays—that of action hero. I blame my mental block on two things. One was the difference in writing styles between the time Doyle's Sherlockian canon was created and now, but the bigger cause was the visual I had in my head of Nigel Bruce's portrayal of Watson. Even though I knew from the canon that Watson wasn't a foolish duffer, I still kept picturing him that way. Even the wonderful Granada Television Sherlock Holmes series, in which both David Burke and Edward Hardwicke played Watson, couldn't shake that stout fellow out of my head. It took the 2009 movie *Sherlock Holmes*, with Jude Law as Watson, to get my attention. First off, there was the fact that Law was a much younger, buffer Watson than I'd ever seen before. He was still reliable and loyal, and by the terminology of the time, a stout fellow, but this Watson was hot!

Then there's the film's plot, which wasn't the usual polite Victorian investigation. There were explosions and fight scenes and all kinds of special effects. The violence didn't throw me—it was a big-budget feature, after all, so I expected them to take some liberties—but Watson's gambling habit took me aback. I'd never pictured the good doctor with a handful of cards and a glass of brandy, cutting loose.

A bit later, in August of 2010, I discovered *Sherlock*, the BBC adaptation from Steven Moffat and Mark Gatiss. I instantly fell in love with this updated version of the Holmes stories, and as much as I adore what Benedict Cumberbatch does with Holmes, I love how Martin Freeman plays Watson even more.

I was particularly struck by a section in the first episode, "A Study in Pink." John has just moved into Baker Street, but before he can even unpack, Sherlock is called away on a case. A moment later, Sherlock returns and the scene goes like this:

> Holmes: You're a doctor. In fact, you're an Army doctor.
>
> Watson: Yes.
>
> Holmes: Any good?
>
> Watson: Very good.
>
> Holmes: Seen a lot of injuries, then. Violent deaths.
>
> Watson: Well, yes.
>
> Holmes: Bit of trouble too, I bet?
>
> Watson: Of course. Yes. Enough for a lifetime, far too much.
>
> Holmes: Want to see some more?
>
> Watson: Oh, God yes.

From that moment on, the two men work together. Now this Watson is still the perfect exposition delivery system and he gives Holmes plenty of opportunities to explain his brilliance, but for the first time, I started seeing Watson as an adrenalin junkie.

There's another section near the end of the episode, and if you haven't seen this, stop reading now because it's a huge spoiler.

Holmes is playing a mental game with a serial killer, and in doing so, puts himself at serious risk. Watson shoots and kills the murderer, but at a distance, and the police don't know who fired the shot. Even Holmes isn't sure at first, but in talking to Lestrade, he describes what kind of person the shooter had to be:

> Holmes: The bullet they just dug out of the wall's from a hand-gun. A kill shot over that distance, from that kind of a weapon, that's a crack shot we're looking for. But not just a marksman,

a fighter. His hands couldn't have shaken at all, so clearly he's accustomed to violence. He didn't fire until I was in immediate danger, though, so strong moral principle. You're looking for a man probably with a history of military service and nerves of steel…

That's when he stops, because he realizes he's just described John Watson to a T. And this version of Watson is eager to chase criminals, undaunted by danger, willing to kill. Now Sherlock can and does do some of this himself. He's brave, he's a crack shot, he fights. But Watson is the soldier, and the fact that he's just shot a man doesn't faze him in the least. Later on in the episode, after Holmes lets Watson know that he's realized he was the sniper, they have this exchange.

Holmes: Are you all right?

Watson: Yes, of course I'm all right.

Holmes: Well, you have just killed a man.

Watson: Yes, I…That's true, isn't it? But he wasn't a very nice man.

Obviously both the movie *Sherlock Holmes* and the TV show *Sherlock* are adaptations, not Doyle's work, but seeing Watson in this new light inspired me to go back to the Sherlockian canon, and I soon realized that both the Jude Law and the Martin Freeman versions of Watson derive from the canonical descriptions. Obviously I'd been missing things—you might say that I'd seen, but I had not observed. It was time for me to start thinking about Watson in a different way.

Take Jude Law's gambling habit, which I wrote off as Hollywood hyperbole. From Watson's first appearance in *A Study in Scarlet*, mention is made of his gambling, and in "The Adventure of the Dancing Men," it's said that Holmes kept Watson's checkbook locked in a drawer to help control his gambling.

Then there's Martin Freeman's post-traumatic stress symptoms. Right up front in *A Study in Scarlet*, it's said that Watson was at Maiwand, which was a dreadful battle during July of 1880. The British forces were outnumbered ten to one, twenty-five hundred to twenty-five thousand. Watson survived the battle, despite a bullet that grazed an artery. While in the hospital for treatment, he came down with enteric fever (which we now call typhoid), and then recovered from that. So obviously, he's tough, but at the beginning of the story, he's still getting over his illness, so we don't see the real Watson until later on, when he's started to interest himself in Holmes' work. The plot in "A Study in Pink" mirrors this extremely well.

Then I started to see clues of Watson's addiction to action that didn't make it to the big or small screen. Again in *A Study in Scarlet*, Inspector Gregson writes Holmes for help. Holmes isn't even sure he'll go. In fact he says, "I am the most incurably lazy devil that ever stood in shoe leather—that is, when the fit is on me, for I can be spry enough at times." It is Watson who encourages him to go, reminding him that he's been waiting for such a chance and pointing out that Gregson is begging for his help. Holmes is convinced, but he wants Watson to come along.

"Get your hat," he said.

"You wish me to come?"

"Yes, if you have nothing better to do." A minute later we were both in a hansom, driving furiously for the Brixton Road.

I don't think it's too big a stretch to say that Holmes could tell that Watson wanted to go along, or that Holmes might not have gone at all without his friend's nudge. It was Watson's craving for action combined with Holmes's realization that he needed somebody in that role that made them partners.

Later on in the book, we're first introduced to Watson's famous revolver. They are awaiting a murderer's appearance when Holmes asks:

"Have you any arms?"

"I have my old service revolver and a few cartridges."

"You had better clean it and load it. He will be a desperate man, and though I shall take him unawares, it is as well to be ready for anything."

Though still quite early in their relationship, Holmes trusts Watson—not just as a doctor or a mental foil, but because he's ready for anything. Once I started looking for them, I found plenty of other examples of Watson's willingness to jump into any situation, but my favorite is from "The Adventure of the Solitary Cyclist." Holmes and Watson are looking for a young woman who is missing and in danger, and are retracing her footsteps down a country road when this happens.

> At the same instant an empty dog-cart, the horse cantering, the reins trailing, appeared round the curve of the road and rattled swiftly towards us. "Block the road! Stop the horse!"

It is Holmes speaking, and it is Watson who instantly does as asked. It's not even shown! The next words in the story are after Watson stops the horse and Holmes says, "That's right." No mention is made of the fact that Watson is willing and able to stop a runaway horse. Holmes takes it for granted.

So clearly Watson doesn't shy away from danger, and craves excitement in his life. Though he's supposed to be making his living as a doctor, he abandons his medical practice every chance he gets.

He also writes about the adventures he shares with Holmes, and you might think that writing is not an action-hero kind of activity, but research shows that most professional writers have strong needs to influence people in the world. (The results are given in more detail in the book *Motivate Your Writing!* by Stephen P. Kelner, Jr., Ph.D.)

So to me at least, the evidence is clear: John H. Watson is a bona fide action hero.

This aspect of Watson has also shown up in other mysteries, whether or not the authors realize it. A few years back, it was noticed that a lot of mysteries and thrillers included characters who came to be known as *kick-ass sidekicks*. Sometimes they're called *psycho sidekicks*, but that's more because of the irresistible alliteration than their actually being psychotic.

Kick-ass sidekicks provide that dangerous edge a detective sometimes needs, often doing what the detective can't or won't. The best known modern example, and the one that most authors would cite as their inspiration, is Hawk in Robert Parker's Spenser series. Other such sidekicks are Robert Crais's Joe Pike, Harlan Coben's Win, Janet Evanovich's Lula and Ranger, and Mouse in Walter Mosley's Easy Rawlins books. For an actual psycho, there's Bubba in Dennis Lehane's Patrick and Angie series. All of these sidekicks are men or women of action, and seem to live for danger.

So the next time you're reading Doyle's stories or one of the terrific Holmes pastiches, or watching any of the adaptations, show Watson some of the respect he's earned. There's been a lot of debate over the years about what the "H" in John H. Watson stands for. Given the way I'm thinking about the man now, instead of Henry or Hamish, I'd like to humbly propose that H. ought to stand for hellraiser.

✗

Leigh Perry is Toni L.P. Kelner in disguise, or maybe vice versa. As Leigh, she writes the Family Skeleton mysteries. As Toni, she's the co-editor of *New York Times* best-selling anthologies with Charlaine Harris. She's also the author of the "Where Are They Now?" mysteries and the Laura Fleming series (all available as e-books and audiobooks), and an Agatha Award winner for short fiction. Leigh/Toni lives north of Boston with her husband, their two daughters, and two guinea pigs.

A STUDY IN CONSISTENCY

HOW THE FIRST SHERLOCK HOLMES STORY PREFIGURED THE REST

By Dan Andriacco

A Study in Scarlet does not generally win, place, or show in the lists of favorite Sherlock Holmes stories. It's not my favorite either. But I was struck in my recent re-reading the entire Canon by the extent to which this first Holmes story prefigured so much that was to follow. Most of what we love about Sherlock Holmes and his world was there in the beginning, and not just in embryonic form.

Let's take a close look now at the story pattern and plot motifs, the character and methods of Sherlock Holmes, the personality of Dr. Watson, and the presence of various other continuing *dramatis personae* who make their debut appearance in *A Study in Scarlet*.

Ronald A. Knox's seminal paper, "Studies in the Literature of Sherlock Holmes," lists eleven elements of the ideal Sherlock Holmes story. Those elements are:

1. a homely Baker Street scene to start, with invaluable personal touches and sometimes a demonstration by the detective or reference by either Holmes or Watson to an untold tale of Sherlock Holmes;

2. the client's statement of the case;

3. energetic personal investigation by Holmes and Watson, often including the famous floor-walk on hands and knees;

4. refutation by Holmes of the Scotland Yard theory;

5. a few stray hints to the police, which they never adopt;

6. Holmes tells the true course of the case to Dr. Watson as he sees it, but is sometimes wrong;

7. questioning of the victim's relatives, dependents, and others, along with visits to the Records Office, and various investigations in disguise;

8. the criminal is caught or exposed;

9. the criminal confesses;

10. Holmes describes the clues and how he followed them; and

11. the conclusion, often involving a quotation from some standard author.

By Monsignor Knox's reckoning, only *A Study in Scarlet* of the stories published up to that time (1911) has all eleven of those elements. But most stories in the Canon have at least five of them, and not the same five. So we see that in *A Study in Scarlet* the pattern of the archetypical Holmes adventure is not only present, it is most completely realized.

There are a couple of other aspects to this inaugural outing of Holmes and Watson that, while perhaps not as typical as the elements already cited, have a distinctively Sherlockian flavor.

For starters, the roots of the crime—as in so many of the stories—lie in the distant past. In this case, that past is in America. The clearest parallel is the last Holmes novel, *The Valley of Fear*, where the entire second half of the book—just as in *A Study in Scarlet*—is made up of a back story set in the United States. I count another six stories with American roots (FIVE, NOBL, YELL, DANC, REDC, THOR). But sometimes the antecedents of the mystery are in another present or former British colony—India in *The Sign of Four* and "The Crooked Man" and Australia in "The Boscombe Valley Mystery," to cite a few obvious examples. In all, I count nineteen adventures—almost one-third of the Canon—in which the past casts a heavy shadow on current events.

One of the most common ways in which this happens is revenge. The revenge motif of *A Study in Scarlet* comes back again and again, and as early as *The Sign of Four*. Surely Jonathan Small is motivated by revenge as much as by greed. Jefferson Hope is the first of several revenge killers or would-be killers who evoke a degree of sympathy on our part, and are usually permitted to die or flee (ABBE, DEVI) or otherwise escape the long arm of the law (CROO, VEIL), or at least its severest judgment (ILLU).

Hope is also the first of many thwarted grooms in the Canon. There are at least ten engagements in the Sherlock Holmes stories that do not come to fruition because of death, scandal, or estrangement.

More important than these frequent plot themes, however, are the character and methods of Sherlock Holmes—for that is what really engages us as readers. And the Holmes whom we meet in *A Study in Scarlet* remains to a remarkable degree nearly unchanged 40 years later in *The Case Book of Sherlock Holmes*. It's almost as if a fiction writer had contrived this. In *Memories and Adventures*, Sir Arthur Conan Doyle, Dr. Watson's literary agent, writes: "To make a real character, one must sacrifice everything to consistency and remember Goldsmith's criticism of Johnson that 'he would make the little fishes talk like whales.'" Conan Doyle says this of Watson, but it applies to Holmes as well.

You probably recall the observation that Sherlock Holmes may not have been killed at the Reichenbach Falls, but was never the same man afterward. I suggest that a close reading of the stories shows that to be untrue. This is not to say that Holmes never changed his mind about anything. The young man who lectured Watson about keeping his brain attic uncluttered in the second chapter of *A Study in Scarlet* later tells Inspector Macdonald in the second chapter of *The Valley of Fear* that "All knowledge comes useful to the detective." However, the essential character, methods, and *Zeitgeist* of Sherlock Holmes are as constant over the years as if it were always 1895—or, rather, 1881.

In that regard, Holmes is like Nero Wolfe and unlike Ellery Queen, to cite two Great Detectives of the Golden Age. Nero Wolfe and his entire W. 35th Street menagerie vary little from *Fer-de-Lance* to *A Family Affair*, a 41-year stretch. Some characters leave the series in dramatic ways and some are added, but Wolfe, Archie, and the feel of the books don't change significantly. On the other hand, the Ellery Queen of his debut novel, *The Roman Hat Mystery* (1929), shares nothing but a name, an address, and a father with the Ellery Queen of the series finale, *A Fine and Private Place* (1971). Ellery evolved over the years from a Philo Vance clone to his own unique and memorable character.

In exploring the character of Holmes, let us *not* start with that remarkable document "Sherlock Holmes—His Limits," drawn up by Dr. Watson in the first days of their acquaintance. We all know that it is notoriously inaccurate. I do not believe, for example, that Holmes's knowledge of literature that enabled him to quote Goethe (SIGN) and George Sand in their original languages, cite George Meredith (BOSC), and carry a pocket Petrarch (BOSC) was a later development. Watson was simply wrong on literature and philosophy, although he got most of the rest of it right—including, for example, Holmes's mastery of boxing and fencing which are alluded to elsewhere (GLOR).

Remember, this was at a time when Watson also wrote "I might have suspected him of being addicted to the use of some narcotic, had not the temperance and cleanliness of his whole life forbidden such a notion." Of course, Watson was wrong about that, too. In the opening pages of *The Sign of Four* we learn that Holmes is indeed a self-poisoner by morphine and cocaine, the famous seven percent solution. Cocaine is mentioned more often than we might think—six times explicitly (SIGN, SCAN, FIVE, TWIS, YELL, MISS) and three times by implication (DYIN, DEVI, CREE)—although we never again see Holmes actually shoot up. By the time of "The Adventure of the Missing Three-Quarter," Watson had weaned him from drug use, but the good doctor knew "the fiend was not dead but sleeping" and the sleep was a light one.

Dismissing Watson's summary list, then, let us consider Holmes when we (and Watson) first meet him in the laboratory at St. Bart's. When Holmes utters those immortal lines, "You have been in Afghanistan, I perceive," Watson wants to know how he knows. Holmes, however, is much more interested in crowing about his new chemical discovery—the Sherlock Homes test for hemoglobin. After explaining the significance, his eyes fairly glittering, "he put his hand over his heart and bowed as if to some applauding crowd conjured up by his imagination."

Already here in chapter one of *A Study in Scarlet* we see both the chemical researches which continue at Baker Street (SIGN, MUSG, IDEN, NAVA, DANC) and the flair for the dramatic which made Holmes such a fine actor. That dramatic impulse is on display again when, to the astonishment of Watson and the Scotland Yarders, he claps the handcuffs on the cabman in the climactic scene of the novel. "Gentlemen," he cries—again, the eyes flashing—"let me introduce you to Mr. Jonathan Hope, murderer of Enoch Drebber and of Joseph Stangerson." In *The Valley of Fear* (chapter six), he explains himself by saying: "Some touch of the artist wells up within me, and calls insistently for a well-staged performance." This penchant for playing to an audience shows up throughout Holmes's career, such as when he lifts a cover off of a plate to reveal the missing naval treaty, or when he holds up a certain small object and announces, "Gentleman, let me introduce you to the famous black pearl of the Borgias."

Holmes is also a bit of a stage magician in these moments, pulling a rabbit out of a hat at the last minute to surprise the audience. He even draws that analogy himself when he says to Watson in chapter four of *A Study in Scarlet*: "You know a conjuror gets no credit once he has explained his trick, and if I show you too much of my method of working, you will come to the conclusion that I am a very ordinary individual after all." But, of course, throughout the Canon Holmes *does* explain and Watson, or the client, or the police official almost always says something like "How absurdly simple!"

Perhaps it would not be going too far to suggest that what we see on display both in the drama and in the need to explain one's methods is a healthy ego. When Holmes tells us in "The Greek Interpreter" that he does not count modesty among the virtues, we are quite ready to believe him. Even though he is young, untested, and standing at the beginning of his career in *A Study in Scarlet*, he makes bold statements such as: "No man lives or has ever lived who has brought the same amount of study and of natural talent to the detection of crime which I have done." Whether that is simply a factual statement—no modesty need apply, remember—or an exaggeration is rather beside the point. This sounds like the Holmes we know.

He even finds the state of crime to be beneath him already at that early juncture. In chapter two, he complains, "There is no crime to detect, or at most, some bungling villainy with a motive so transparent that even a Scotland Yard official can see through it." It's as though he's yearning for a worthy opponent, a master villain with whom to do battle. He makes similar comments elsewhere before the rise of Professor Moriarty (BOSC, COPP), though perhaps we remember best those complaints post-Reichenbach (NORW, BRUCE) about how dull London has become after the Professor's demise.

A high appreciation of his own talents leads Holmes to a career-long pattern of making ironically deprecating comments to others. At the very beginning of the Lauriston Gardens Mystery (chapter three), he raises his eyebrows sardonically and tells Tobias Gregson, "With two men such as yourself and Lestrade upon the ground, there will not be much for a third party to find out." A few pages later he declines to give the officials his view of the case, offering the sarcastic reason, "You are doing so well now that it would be a pity for anyone to interfere."

This calls to mind a wonderfully snarky exchange with Lestrade during the Boscombe Valley Mystery. "I find it hard enough to tackle facts, Holmes, without flying away after theories and fancies," says the official detective. "You are right," responds Holmes, "you do find it very hard to tackle the facts." Years later, welcomed back to London by Lestrade after the Great Hiatus, Holmes says, "But you handled the Molesy Mystery with less than your usual— that's to say, you handled it fairly well (EMPT)."

Regrettably, this attitude of condescension is not reserved solely for the official police. At times it is extended to the faithful Watson as well—especially in the later stories. My favorite sardonic line directed against the good doctor comes in "The Adventure of the Three Students," wherein Holmes says, "Watson, I have always done you an injustice. There are others." In somewhat the same mean spirit, at the beginning of *The Valley of Fear*, Watson says, "I am inclined to think–" and Holmes interrupts him with "I should certainly do so."

In *A Study in Scarlet*, the relationship between Holmes and Watson is just getting started. Watson is not yet one of the few people to whom Holmes ever applies the term "friend," along with Victor Trevor and—surprisingly "friend Lestrade." And how does young Holmes treat the near-stranger Watson in these early days? Pretty much the same way he treats him for the next forty years. In chapter three, for example, Holmes explains how he deduced—induced, really—that the man who delivered a letter from Tobias Gregson was a retired sergeant of marines. That provokes this exchange:

"Wonderful!" I ejaculated.

"Commonplace," said Holmes, though I thought from his expression that he was pleased at my evident surprise and admiration.

It is not until "A Scandal in Bohemia" that Holmes says "I am lost without my Boswell," but *A Study in Scarlet* already shows us how much the actor needs an audience and adulation. Watson, of course, is always there to provide it, as in the very next chapter of *A Study in Scarlet* when he exclaims, "You amaze me, Holmes!" A computer would have a nervous breakdown trying to calculate the number of times similar dialogue is repeated in the other fifty-nine stories. (In "The Adventure of the Crooked Man," you will recall, Holmes's response to "Wonderful!" is the famous "Elementary.")

When Holmes takes delivery of that letter from Tobias Gregson mentioned a moment ago, he does a curious thing which he does again and again throughout the Canon: He asks Watson to read it to him out loud. (See SCAN, IDEN, STOC, NORW, CARD.) Was Sherlock Holmes illiterate? One scholar thought so, but there are ample instances of Holmes reading on his own. Think of all the newspapers he studied while briefing himself on the case of Silver Blaze, for example. Also, on numerous occasions Holmes consults the clippings in his commonplace books. And in *The Valley of Fear* he looks up words in Whitaker's Almanac all by himself. No, I think we can assume that Sherlock Holmes could read, but chose not to. He'd rather have Watson do it for him.

Another habit of Holmes which started in *A Study in Scarlet* was asking Watson to bring a gun, which he does in chapter five as they await the person who answered Holmes's advert. "Put your pistol in your pocket," he says. Why doesn't he put a pistol in his own pocket? We know that Holmes has one because he uses it to shoot a patriotic V.R. on the wall of the sitting room (MUSG). He even carries it on a case once in a while (GREE, BERY, FINA, SOLI). But in many stories (REDH, SPEC, SIXN, EMPT, 3GAR, THOR, BRUC) he asks Watson to bring his revolver—presumably that famous Eley's No. 2.

I think it's clear that Holmes quickly learned to lean on Watson for everything from reading to gun-toting. We might even say that he takes advantage of him. No wonder Rex Stout theorized that

"Watson Was a Woman," and actually Mrs. Sherlock Holmes. Of course we know that Stout's charming speculation cannot be true because Holmes late in his career accuses the doctor of being self-ish by deserting him for a wife (BLAN). The nerve of that Watson!

Just as Holmes's character changes little over the years, so do his investigative techniques. With one major exception, they are all on display in *A Study in Scarlet*.

The basic Holmes approach of observation and induction—which he always inaccurately called *de*duction—is laid out in his article "The Book of Life:" "By a man's finger-nails, [Holmes writes] by his coat sleeve, by his boot, by his trouser knees, by the callosities of his forefinger and thumb, by his shirt-cuffs—by each of these a man's calling is plainly revealed." No, Watson, that is not "ineffable twaddle!" It would be tedious to go through the Canon citing later examples in which Holmes draws conclusions from each of these, but one need go no further than "The Adventure of the Red-headed League" to recall what Holmes was able to tell about Jabez Wilson—and about his assistant with the worn trouser knees. In later stories Holmes will say that nothing is so important as trifles (TWIS) and that his method is founded on the observance of trifles (BOSC).

Equally central to the Holmes method is the process of elimination. Holmes does not yet say, "When you have eliminated the impossible, whatever remains—however improbable—must be the truth." That wording appears in *The Sign of Four* and later tales (BERY, BRUC, BLAN). But the *process* is used here and in every story in which Holmes actually does detective work. In describing his conclusion that Enoch Drebber had been forcibly administered poison, Holmes says, "By the method of exclusion I had arrived at this result, for no other hypothesis would meet the facts." Isn't that what he does all the time?

Another important notion is that the idea that the "the most commonplace crime is often the most mysterious," as he says in chapter seven of part one of *A Study in Scarlet.* The same concept is approached from another viewpoint in "The Adventure of the Red-headed League" and other stories (HOUN, REDH), where he says the more bizarre or outré a case is, the easier it is to solve.

These foundational techniques and principles are essentially present in every Sherlock Holmes story, whether explicitly referred to or not. In addition, I have identified eight important techniques that Holmes used throughout his career, of which he uses seven in his first investigation with Dr. Watson. (I do not include burglary among the eight because it is only used three times—MILV, BRUC, RETI). Let's take these frequently used techniques one by one:

Technique (1): Analogy or reference to previous cases, either from Holmes's encyclopedic memory for crime or from his commonplace books. In the first chapter of *A Study in Scarlet*, he mentions so many cases that Stamford suggests he start a newspaper called "Police News of the Past." At the end of the case, explaining the solution to Watson, Holmes sites two cases of forcible administration of poison which, he says, "would occur to any toxicologist."

(How odd, by the way, that he never calls attention to the parallels in his own cases. Should not "The Three Garridebs" or "The Stock-Broker's Clerk" have reminded him of "The Red-Headed League," "The Six Napoleons" of "The Blue Carbuncle," and "The Second Stain" of "The Naval Treaty?" And how about the parallel between *The Valley of Fear* and "The Norwood Builder?" But I digress.)

Interestingly, while Holmes's dependence on his knowledge of criminal history doesn't change, his way of describing it does. In the third chapter of the first book, he quotes the Bible: "There is nothing new under the sun. It has all been done before." In the second chapter of his last book-length adventure, *The Valley of Fear*, Holmes sounds rather Buddhist instead: "The old wheel turns and the same spoke comes up," he says. "It's all been done before, and will be again."

Technique (2): Music, either at the concert the hall or provided by his own violin. Music was an aid to his cases and not an escape from them, it seems to me. Holmes hints at this in "The Red-Headed League" when he says the German music on the concert hall program "is introspective, and I want to introspect." In *A Study in Scarlet*, Holmes enjoys a concert by Norman-Néruda as well as his own violin playing.

Technique (3): Advertising. The ad for a wedding ring found in the Brixton Road (chapter five) is the first of seven occasions throughout the Canon in which Holmes uses a newspaper ad on a case. Nero Wolfe did this a lot, too. Like father, like son?

Technique (4): On-scene investigation or, in a few cases, legwork such as visiting a records office. This is how Holmes gathers data, which is all-important. "It is a capital mistake to theorize before one has data," he says early in *A Study in Scarlet*. As the Oxford edition of the Canon notes, variations of this maxim appear in six other tales (CARD, REIG, ABBE, SECO, WIST, SUSS).

Technique (5): Following the suspect or someone else. In this broad category I include both surveillance and tracking, and both occur in *A Study in Scarlet*. The tracking is made easier by the fact that the murderer wore square-toed boots. It is a curious matter that quite often when Holmes tracks someone that person is wearing square-toed boots (RESI), and yet Holmes generally acts as if this footwear were unusual and therefore easy to follow.

Technique (6): The Baker Street Irregulars. These lads go where Holmes and Watson cannot, and there are more of them. They make their debut in chapter six of *A Study in Scarlet* and also appear in *The Sign of Four* (where they are called irregulars for the first time), and in "The Crooked Man."

Technique (7): Tobacco. This is helpful not only in three-pipe problems (REDH), but in less complicated ones as well. "Of the 60 cases, only 4 are without some reference to smoking," according to Steve Doyle and David A. Crowder (*Sherlock Holmes for Dummies*, p. 204). In addition to smoking tobacco, Holmes also looked to it for clues. In *A Study in Scarlet*, identifying the ash of a Trichinopoly cigar provides the occasion for Holmes to tell Watson that he has written a monograph on cigar ashes—one of at least eleven works of Sherlock Holmes from "The Book of Life" to *The Practical Handbook of Bee Culture*. In *The Sign of Four* we learn that this monograph describes 140 different tobacco ashes. In "The Adventure of the Golden Pince-Nez," Holmes scatters cigarette ashes on the floor to detect footprints.

All of the above techniques appear in *A Study in Scarlet*. The only major method used throughout his career that does *not* appear here is:

Technique (8): Disguise. Holmes is such a master of disguise that he even fools Watson on several occasions (SIGN, TWIS, FINA, EMPT). Closely allied to this is the use of an alias, a false pretense, or a pretended illness. The only disguise in *A Study in Scarlet* is used *against* Holmes in chapter five, causing him to cry,

"We were the old women to be fooled." Remember, to argue that the world of Sherlock Holmes is remarkably consistent is not to say that there are *no* changes.

There is, however, "one fixed point in a changing age"—Dr. John H. Watson, M.D., late of the Army Medical Department. From page one of *A Study in Scarlet* he is "a man of action," as Holmes calls him in *The Hound of the Baskervilles*. By chapter three he is the admiring companion. In chapter four, after another cry of amazement early in the chapter, he goes on to say, "I am rather in the dark still." That's our Watson! So is the loyal friend who, at the end of the story, vows to write up the adventure so that the world's first consulting detective will get the credit he deserves. In "The Adventure of the Dying Detective," when Holmes is pretending to be talking out of his head, the one true statement is when he tells Watson, "You never did fail me."

For all of this we can forgive him the minor eccentricity of his Jezail bullet wound—which seemed to travel from his arm in *A Study in Scarlet* to his leg in *The Sign of Four* before Watson just gave up and located it "in one of my limbs" in "The Adventure of the Noble Bachelor."

In the second chapter of *A Study in Scarlet*, he and Holmes take up rooms together at 221B Baker Street, London—surely one of the most famous addresses in the world, and one to which their names are forever linked.

Their landlady is never named in *A Study in Scarlet*, but undoubtedly she is Mrs. Hudson from the beginning (whoever Mrs. Turner in "A Scandal in Bohemia" may be), just as surely as Lestrade and Gregson climb those seventeen steps to 221B in the very first story.

Although many other Scotland Yard officials make their appearance in the Canon—particularly young Stanley Hopkins in the later years—Lestrade and Gregson remain the archetypical inspectors. They may not have the grip on the popular imagination of Mycroft or Moriarty, but they appear far more often in the Canon than the two M's. Lestrade appears or is alluded to in thirteen stories, with the latest being "The Adventure of the Three Garridebs" in 1902. Gregson is in five stories, including the first two.

The attitude of the official police toward Holmes does change over the years, ranging from denial that they need him in *A Study in Scarlet* to praise in later years. By "The Adventure of the Six Napoleons," Lestrade says "we're proud of you at the Yard," and in "The Adventure of the Empty House" he willingly admits "It's good to see you back in London, sir." Gregson is equally fulsome when he says in "The Adventure of the Red Circle," "I was never in a case yet that I didn't feel stronger with you at my side."

And so we see that not only were the characters of Holmes and Watson, and the detective's methods, largely established full-blown in their very first adventure, but so was what we might call the Baker Street scene—the setting and the minor members of the troupe. And in the immortal words of Vincent Starrett (albeit not his most famous):

> Shall they not always live in Baker Street? Are they not there as one writes?...Outside the hansoms rattle through the rain, and Moriarty plans his latest deviltry. Within, the sea coal flames upon the hearth and Holmes and Watson take their well-won ease...So they still live for all that love them well: in a romantic chamber of the heart, in a nostalgic country of the mind, where it is always 1895.

Dan Andriacco has been reading Sherlock Holmes for half a century. His eight books all nod toward Holmes, including a recent collection of shorter mysteries, *Rogues Gallery*. Dan also writes a popular blog, *Baker Street Beat*, which was also the name of his first book.

SHERLOCK HOLMES AND THE AUTUMN OF TERROR

by J.G. Grimmer

31 October, 1888: 221B Baker Street

It was the worst year for my friend and me. The unspeakable acts committed by the Whitechapel butcher now known as "Jack the Ripper" were the news of the day.

"Watson, I've reread the letter the Ripper sent to *The Times* and believe that I've deduced an insight," Sherlock Holmes said.

I emptied my pipe into the ashtray and squinted through the haze produced by the copious amount of smoke made by our pipes. "Oh? What is that, Holmes? Have you discovered the lunatic's identity?"

My friend took a long draw from his pipe and blew out a noxious cloud created by shag tobacco when ignited by flame, a grin on his face. "Hardly—no, the insight points to character type."

"Oh," I replied.

Holmes stood at the window looking at the hustle and bustle of Baker Street, so lost in his thoughts that he forgot we were having a conversation, or so I thought.

"*And?*" I prompted him.

"Forgive me, dear fellow," he said contritely. "Yes, the writing suggests a crude intellect, but I believe it is a mask concealing something more."

"What?"

"The truth—a truth I fear is far more terrible than can be imagined."

I raised my eyebrows. "I repeat, *what is that?*"

"I fear that the Ripper is not the madman he is made out to be."

Holmes annoyed me to no end when he did this. And he *knew* it. I was about to tell him so when there was a knock at the door. I rose and opened it to reveal Holmes's older brother Mycroft.

"Doctor," he grumbled perfunctorily and waddled toward his brother. "I cannot imagine what could keep you so occupied that you would allow this wholesale slaughter to continue."

Holmes put his pipe on the mantel without emptying it only to pick up a cigar and light it. "Mycroft, that is sheer nonsense! I've offered my help to the Yard, and it was rejected by everyone from Inspector Lestrade to Sir Charles Warren himself."

I nodded my assent as Mycroft settled his large frame on the leather chair. "That may well be," he said, "and yet I am offering you the opportunity to put this ghastly business to an end."

"Indeed?" Holmes said. "On whose authority am I presented with this opportunity?"

Mycroft shifted in the chair. "I cannot say."

"Cannot or *will* not?"

"That is irrelevant. Do you accept?"

"Of course. Who shall I report to?"

Mycroft raised an eyebrow. "*Me.*"

Sherlock smiled. "Of course."

Mycroft rose from the chair. "I shall be expecting a report soon—might I suggest tomorrow?"

"You will have it, "Holmes replied. "Will you receive it here?"

Mycroft exhaled sharply. "Certainly not!" he exclaimed. "At the Diogenes Club. Until tomorrow."

I opened the door for him.

"Thank you, Doctor," he said cordially and departed.

Holmes returned to the window and watched Mycroft's carriage make its way down Baker Street. "What do you make of this?" he asked.

"I don't know," I replied. "It must be of great importance to your brother. He rarely leaves his club."

"Agreed," Holmes said, removing his smoking jacket. "Time to go to work."

Before I could speak, he disappeared into the room that served as his laboratory, which was filled with vials, tubes, and beakers from which emanated the vilest odors that gave our landlady, Mrs Hudson, fits. I shrugged my shoulders, knowing that once that door was shut, Holmes would be as isolated as any cloister. So I picked up a copy of *The Times*, sat down, and commenced to read.

Sometime later, a knock on the door woke me. Groggily I made my way to it. "Holmes?" I said.

"No, it's me," Mrs Hudson said from the other side. "I thought you two would like something to eat."

I opened the door and in bustled Mrs Hudson carrying a tray. She set it down, wiped her hands on her apron, and looked around.

"Where's Mr Holmes?" she asked.

I went to the door to the laboratory. "Holmes?" I called and knocked, then opened it only to find the room empty. "Did you see him, Mrs Hudson?"

"No, there hasn't been a sound since his brother left hours ago. Well, you'd better eat, Doctor. Shepherd's Pie cools quickly enough, and who knows where Mr Holmes has got to." She took one of the covered plates and left.

"Thank you." I called after her and closed the door. *Yes indeed,* I thought while eating—*where are you Holmes?*

31 October, 1888, Eleven p.m., Whitechapel:

Holmes assumed the appearance and dress of a common labourer and would have been unidentifiable, even by his own brother. The thread-bare clothes, the grime under his fingernails, the dirt on his face, and the appearance of teeth uncared for for years were the perfect camouflage—and would have to be if he were to be accepted by the slum denizens as one of their own.

He began his reconnaissance in the area of Berner Street and Mitre Square where the infamous "double event" occurred on 30 September, with the murders of Elizabeth "Long Liz" Stride and Catherine Eddowes. Even at this late hour, the streets were alive with labourers going to and from the factories, and rich young men in top hats and tails cruising to sample the forbidden pleasures offered by women undeterred by morality. These unfortunates were driven not by lust, but by the simple desire to have enough money for a bed and perhaps food at some dilapidated lodging house.

From the lurid accounts of the murders in the press, Holmes surmised that the Ripper struck between the hours of midnight and six a.m. From that it followed that this area would be familiar to the killer, who might well be somewhere here now seeking out his next unfortunate victim.

Holmes leaned against a grimy, soot-covered wall, filled a clay pipe, lit it, and surveyed the pathetic people passing before him. *Poor devils*, he thought, yet always mindful that these were human beings who loved and laughed, whose children played, all trying to go through their lives as best they could despite the cruel trick Fate or Providence played on them.

The hours passed and except for a drunken brawl, the sounds of domestic strife, and children crying, nothing happened as the sky began to brighten.

1 November, 1888, seven a.m., 221 B Baker Street:

Holmes entered his rooms without waking anyone and fell gratefully into bed.

I rose at eight a.m. and was relieved to see that the door to Holmes' room was closed. I could only imagine where he'd been the entire evening—Whitechapel obviously—and whatever he discovered would be related to me at his leisure. Before breakfast I dressed and set out for my morning walk. When I returned at nine a.m., Mrs Hudson informed me that Holmes had left, "without so much as a morsel," she said.

When I inquired if he had told her where he was going, she replied, "his brother's club." I ate breakfast alone and read to pass the time as I had no patients to see. Holmes arrived at midday with a bundle of folders under his arm.

"Sorry to wake you, Watson."

"What? I wasn't sleeping," I replied indignantly. "You startled me, coming and going at all hours."

He set the stack down on the table. "My apologies, dear fellow."

I straightened in my chair. "Where have you been?"

"You mean this morning?"

"You know very well I mean this morning and last evening."

Holmes sat down and opened a folder. "I was in Whitechapel until six this morning. I returned by seven, slept until eight-thirty, and left for Mycroft's club at eight-forty-five, just missing your arrival. I was at the Diogenes Club until my return a few moments ago."

"I noticed that the folders you have there have H-Division written on them—would that be the Yard's homicide detectives?"

Holmes clapped his hands. "Well done, Watson."

"Elementary," I replied. "Have you discovered anything?"

"About the Ripper, I'm afraid not, however I did witness the most appalling squalor in Whitechapel, Watson. Something must be done to improve the lot of those poor souls, especially the children."

"I couldn't agree with you more. The Charity Hospitals I've visited there are a step in the right direction, providing excellent care to the people who are in need."

"I'm glad to hear that," Holmes said. "By the way, next time you go to one could you discreetly inquire among your colleagues if they've treated any women who may have heard anything?"

"Of course."

Holmes nodded. "Could you also measure how your colleagues respond?"

"Why? You don't suspect a doctor is responsible—*do you*?"

Holmes filled a pipe, a straight, short-stemmed affair. "I'm terribly sorry to tread upon the conventions of your profession, dear fellow, but I suspect everyone. Yes, even a physician may be capable of these deeds, ghastly as they are. Don't forget, Watson, the mark of Cain is upon us all."

"Very well," I consented, "However, I find it highly improbable that any man who swore the Hippocratic Oath could possibly be the Ripper."

Holmes made no reply. Instead he puffed on his pipe and turned his attention to the open folder on his lap.

The very idea, I thought as I picked up the latest edition of the *Medical Journal* and ignited the tobacco in my pipe.

"Watson?"

I looked up. "Yes, Holmes?"

"Shouldn't you be going?"

"Now?"

"Certainly, there's no time to lose. We must catch this killer. If you leave now, you'll be back in time for supper."

I put down the journal, sighed, got up and took my coat and hat from the rack and opened the door. "You're right. What are you going to do?"

Holmes looked down at the stack of folders at his feet. "I have these police reports to go through, and then I'll have some tea and lunch and perhaps take a nap before supper."

"Oh," I replied, looked twice at him, and then left. On the street I hailed a hansom cab.

"Where to?" the driver asked.

"The Charity Hospital in Whitechapel, my good man. And hurry, please."

The driver doffed his cap. "Right you are, sir. I'll have you there in good time."

It was a bleak, cold grey afternoon. I shivered and drew my coat tightly around me. As we drove through the streets of the West End a sudden change came over the cityscape; the carefully maintained and elegant offices, residences, church edifices, and swept streets gave way to desolate fallow fields, and huddled-close-together filthy tenement buildings—many with broken windows which were covered by burlap sacks, or whatever the occupants could find to keep the cold air, wind, and rain out. The cab drove through steam rising out of open gutters and by the workhouses where so many who have no trade, profession, or social standing must nonetheless provide lodging and food for themselves and their children. Their only other choice is to beg on the streets for their daily bread and live in some alley.

Her Majesty is a kind, compassionate monarch. Surely she is told that such squalid conditions exist. And if not, I thought as the cab bucked and swayed over the neglected pavement—why not? The cab halted abruptly in front of the hospital.

"Whitechapel Charity Hospital," the driver announced, opening the door for me.

I stepped down and placed the fare in his dirty hand, which remained open.

He cleared his throat. "Didn't I say I'd get ya here in good time?"

My watch was in my waistcoat pocket, and I wasn't about to expose myself to the wintry conditions—besides, I didn't time the trip in any event. "So you did," I replied and swiftly went up the stairs to the entrance. As I reached the doors, I heard him mumble.

"Bloody doctors, they're all alike."

I turned and cast a disapprovingly raised eyebrow at him, but he was already driving away. Bloody hansom drivers, I thought watching him. You put yourself in their hands, and they shake you as if you're a salt shaker, and then they have the audacity to expect you to tip them! "Hmmmp!" I said, irritated, and entered the hospital. It was organized by a consortium of physicians who donated their time and gifts to heal those who could not pay.

I talked to several colleagues and gleaned very little, other than quotes such as "bloody business," and "the man should be locked away in Bedlam," but as to treating the Ripper's victims or any of their friends—nothing. Naturally they treated prostitutes, but did not engage such persons in idle conversation. An altogether proper attitude to be sure, but not much help in a murder investigation.

As I made my way toward the exit, the door opened and in walked Inspectors Abberline and Lestrade, no doubt pursuing the same line of reasoning. Fortunately, I recognized them before they recognized me, and swiftly turned my back to them to consult the clock. I did not know Inspector Frederick Abberline beyond what was reported in the press and that he was in charge of the Ripper investigation. If recognized by Lestrade, I would have been hard pressed to explain my presence, since *he* knows that my practice is private.

Without looking back, I made my way out and hailed the first hansom that came by. I returned to our lodgings just before three, and found Holmes seated, fingers steepled, eyes closed, and the stack of police reports on the floor to the right of his chair. I hung up my hat, scarf, and coat and sat in the chair facing him. I knew that my friend was deep in thought, that amazing mind sifting through every detail that was found in those reports. As I settled in, his eyes opened.

"Ah, Watson. What did you learn?"

"Very little, I'm afraid."

He nodded. "Just as I suspected. I on the other hand have learned a very great deal."

I let his sarcastic aside pass. "Do tell."

"The police have eight suspects who couldn't be more disparate; everyone from John Netley, a carriage driver, and Aaron Kosminsky, a Polish Jew—to the likes of Doctor Sir William Gull, the Queen's physician, and His Royal Highness Prince Albert Victor Christian Edward, or 'Eddy' as Her Majesty's grandson is known."

"Really?" I exclaimed. "Good God!"

"That's not all," Holmes said. "The list is rounded off by an American actor, Richard Mansfield, a clairvoyant named Robert James Lees, Doctor Montague John Druitt, Doctor Gull's son-in-law, and finally Michael Ostrong, a Russian doctor and convict."

"Which of them is the Ripper?"

"None."

"*None?*"

"That's right, old friend. The police have pursued nearly every conceivable theory no matter how remote, or in some cases, utterly ludicrous it may be. As a result, the Ripper is still free."

I thought about this for a moment. "What are we to do?"

"Precisely what we are doing, Watson. We must make haste, though; I do not believe we have much time before the Ripper disappears forever."

There was a knock at the door. I rose from my chair. Holmes did as well, evidence that he did not know who it was. I opened the door, and to my horror in walked Inspector Lestrade, who nodded at Holmes.

"Ah, Lestrade," Holmes said, "What can I do for you?"

"Nothing, Mr Holmes," Lestrade replied, and I felt a chill at the back of my neck. "Actually, I'm here to ask Doctor Watson some questions."

"Watson?" Holmes asked.

"Yes," Lestrade said, "I saw him at the Charity Hospital this afternoon. Inspector Abberline and I went there to question the doctors and their patients in connection with this bloody business."

"Indeed?" Holmes asked.

"Yes, Doctor Watson turned his back to us as we walked in, apparently to look at the time, but obviously in an effort to evade us. Now then, Doctor, I did not mention that I knew you to Inspector Abberline, but since I know that your practice is strictly private I was wondering why were you there?"

I was keenly aware that both men were looking at me intently. "Well, I…"

Lestrade waved his hand. "No need, Doctor, it is obvious why you were there." He turned his policeman's gaze on Holmes. "I believe that you were told you were not needed on this case."

Unperturbed, Holmes replied. "Someone wants my services, Lestrade."

"Who?" Lestrade asked, through squinted eyes.

"Sorry, I am not at liberty to say." Holmes replied, discreetly positioning himself to block the stack of reports from Lestrade's view.

"I see," Lestrade said, turned and made his way to the door. "Well, I'll be on my way."

"Goodbye, Inspector," Holmes called after him.

Lestrade nodded to us both and left.

"He gave up rather easily, didn't he?" I asked.

Holmes shook his head. "Lestrade's enough of an investigator to know that I've been retained by someone in authority, and that he should not press the issue."

"I see," I said, although I really didn't.

We spent the remainder of the afternoon, including supper in the privacy of our own thoughts. Afterward, Holmes announced that he was going to Mycroft's club, and not to expect him home until morning. For the next seven weeks, every evening Holmes would persevere in his vigil among the denizens of Whitechapel, interacting with them in a variety of disguises: from a dock worker to a common labourer, from a slaughterhouse butcher to a pimp. Although they accepted him as one of their own, he was no closer to solving the Ripper murders. The fact that no murders occurred in that time was little consolation to my friend, who, exhausted and demoralized, wanted to bring this killer to justice to the point of obsession that rivaled his pursuit of Moriarty.

9 November, 1888

Disguised as a workhouse labourer, Holmes left our lodgings for Whitechapel, just as he had all the evenings previously. He took up position in an alley near Dorset Street in Miller's Court, a grimy cul-de-sac containing small threadbare apartments. At approximately two a.m. he observed a man and woman entering the cul-de-sac as had others earlier; however, there was something inexplicably odd about the man who, unlike the others, was well dressed in black evening clothes with a top hat, and he carried a walking stick with a large heavy handle that looked like silver.

Although his face was in shadow, Holmes sensed a disfigurement of the features that caused the hair on the back of his neck to stand on end. At three a.m. Holmes heard a woman's cry, but he had heard many cries, along with shouting, and babies wailing throughout the night. At four-fifteen a.m. he heard a door open close by, and footsteps as the well-dressed man emerged.

Holmes watched him as he walked to the corner and stopped.

The man turned suddenly to face in Holmes's direction, as if aware that he was being watched. Even though his face was still hidden by shadow, Holmes knew that the man was looking directly at him. The hair on the back of Holmes's neck stood up again when the strange man pointed his stick at him.

The woman! Holmes impulsively ran into the cul-de-sac, his eyes sweeping the windows of each apartment. They were all dark, except one which was lit by the glow from what Holmes surmised to be a fireplace. He rushed to it and peered inside. What he saw looked like the anteroom to Hell. Lit by the flickering yellow light from the fireplace was the horribly butchered body of a woman, mutilated nearly beyond recognition. Sickened and horrified, Holmes desperately wanted to look away, and although this took but a few seconds it seemed to Holmes an eternity.

Finally he turned away, making note of the address—26 Dorset—and saw the strange man still standing at the corner. The two stared at each other, then the man tipped his hat, and in a flash of his cloak turned and disappeared into the fog.

"Stop!" Holmes shouted, and bolted after him.

The man Holmes now knew to be the Ripper was swift and agile, but his gait seemed simian in nature, as if he were not a man but some great ape. They rounded a corner approaching the affluent West End when the Ripper collided with a patrolman sending both hard to the pavement. The Ripper growled, and as he rolled to get up Holmes was on top of him, locking one arm behind his back.

"There's no escape," Holmes said.

The Ripper turned to him and Holmes's face went white as he beheld the distorted countenance. The eyes were wild and red-rimmed, yet there was considerable intelligence behind them. The Ripper smiled—a smile that was pure evil. "Ah, but there is," he said, and despite the hold on him threw Holmes off with astonishing ease and was running once again.

The patrolman was regaining consciousness as Holmes got to his feet and disappeared into the mist. Holmes caught sight of the Ripper just as he turned onto a side street, and followed him. Holmes watched in fascination as the small man leapt over a low brick wall and down into a stairwell, and was down the stairs just as the door slammed in front of him. Holmes went around the block to the front entrance and after a moment to compose himself, he knocked at the door again and again until it opened revealing a haggard looking butler.

"I'm Sherlock Holmes, is your master at home?"

"Do you know what time it is, *sir*? Of course he is!"

"Wake him please, I just witnessed a man breaking in the rear entrance, and believe you are all in danger."

The poor man sighed, his shoulders sank.

"May I come in?"

"Oh, forgive me, sir, of course." The butler led Holmes in and shut the door.

"We must wake your master and call the police."

"One moment, sir," the butler replied and rushed up the stairs. He returned a few moments later. "He's not here, Mr Holmes, but he's been keeping very odd hours of late."

"Show me to that back room. If your master's there, he is in grave danger."

They arrived at the door only to find it locked. From within they were startled to hear what sounded like animal noises and glass breaking. The frail-looking butler threw himself against the door.

"I'll take care of this," Holmes said. "Call the police."

"Yes, sir," the butler replied, and walked away rubbing his shoulder.

Holmes was about to break the door down when the noises from inside abruptly stopped, then the doorknob turned and the door swung open revealing a disheveled-looking man wearing a white coat much like the kind doctors wear.

"Who are you?" he asked in a quiet voice.

"Sherlock Holmes. Are you all right?"

The man ran fingers through his hair. "Yes, yes I think so."

"Where is the other man?"

"Gone."

"Gone?"

"Yes, when he heard you at the door he simply left."

Holmes regarded the pale man closely; both he and the room appeared to have been through a struggle that left a lot of glass broken and furniture turned over, and there was something very disturbing about his eyes—something familiar.

By this time, the butler returned with a patrolman.

"Oh, Doctor, I am ever so glad to see you! Are you all right?" the butler said.

"Yes, Poole, I was working late."

"What's going on here?" the patrolman asked.

"There's been a break-in, officer," the butler said. "Mr Holmes here witnessed the crime."

"Mr Holmes, eh?" the officer asked, squinting.

"Yes, I'm Sherlock Holmes, but I wasn't pursuing a burglar, I was pursuing the Ripper."

"The Ripper?" the patrolman asked. "Are you certain, Mr Holmes?"

"I am."

"Where is he, then?" the patrolman asked, looking around the damaged room.

"He escaped," the doctor replied.

"Which way did he go?" the patrolman inquired.

"Out the back door," the doctor replied.

"Well then, we're wasting valuable time," the patrolman said, starting for the door.

"Hold on a moment," Holmes said, intently searching the doctor's eyes.

"Why?" the patrolman asked.

"I don't know how you did this, Doctor, but we both know where the Ripper went," Holmes said, and by the doctor's expression he knew he was right.

"What are you talking about, Mr Holmes?" the patrolman asked. "I know this man—he's Doctor Henry Jekyll."

"Indeed he is," the butler added.

"That may well be, gentlemen, but this is our man. They say the eyes are the mirror of the soul, Doctor Jekyll. I never subscribed to that notion until tonight. Also you're still wearing the same boots and trousers as the murderer; obviously you did not have time to change them."

Jekyll looked squarely at Holmes. "Poole, get Mr Holmes a brandy. He obviously is not feeling well."

"No, thank you," Holmes said. "Officer, I know how this appears, but this man is the Ripper."

"I've read some of your exploits in the *Strand*, Mr Holmes, and admired your use of deductive logic and reasoning—but this. Evidently your chronicler has exaggerated somewhat," Jekyll said.

"Come along now, Mr Holmes," the patrolman said.

"Tell them, Jekyll. For the sake of your soul tell them what you've done."

"I've done nothing," Jekyll said. "I'm Doctor Henry Jekyll—I *am* Doctor Henry Jekyll."

While he was speaking, what best could be described as a shadow crossed Jekyll's face, and his brow thickened. Another shadow swept across leaving in its wake more grotesque changes, as the eyebrows became so prodigious that they met over the nose which broadened, the nostrils flaring. A final shadow darkened Jekyll's distorted countenance, and when it passed they were astonished to behold a completely different man—with a widow's peak, a brow that hung over wild, red-rimmed eyes, and teeth which had been enlarged and stretched the lips and mouth into a cruel perpetual grin.

"Jekyll," Holmes whispered.

"Jekyll's dead—I'm Hyde." This statement, more than the metamorphosis, chilled all who heard it to the core. With a growl Hyde lunged at Holmes, his oversized hands closed quickly around my friend's throat. A shot rang out. Then another, and another, and Hyde slumped to the floor where he breathed his last in two sharp gasps.

Holmes gasped, pocketing his revolver.

Poole crossed himself, and Holmes regarded Hyde, whose contorted features remained—a testament to the evil life to which Jekyll had succumbed.

221 B Baker Street, London. Epilogue:

A complete report of these events was made to Mycroft, which were then burned along with all of Jekyll's notes that detailed his vile experiments.

The body of Hyde was cremated, the ashes carried by the four winds into oblivion. It was decided at the highest levels that the identity of "Jack the Ripper" would never be known. If the truth of Jekyll's experiments into the darkness of Man were ever revealed—what would become of us?

"As if we could rid ourselves of Hyde that easily," Holmes observed.

✗

"PSST, WANNA BUY SOME HOT MYSTERIES?"

THE ADVENTURE OF THE OLD RUSSIAN WOMAN

by Jack Grochot

Pitch dark settled in by the time Sherlock Holmes and I finished a fine fish dinner at Simpson's, our favourite restaurant, and we walked at a leisurely pace from the Strand to our Baker Street apartment, talking about the recent successful conclusion of an investigation into a domestic complication involving Mrs Cecil Forrester, the erstwhile client. "If I had my way, Watson," Holmes remarked, "her husband would have been dragged before his fellow members of Parliament and forced to admit his role in the corruption scandal. But, instead, she chose to sweep his participation under the rug and protect his seat, a source of income from which she too has reaped benefits. I was tempted to tip off one of my connections in the press, rather than keep mum and let the matter wither on the vine."

"But if you had dropped a hint to the newspapers, that would have violated your pledge of confidentiality," I proposed.

"That is the clincher, my good man," he answered. "It is what has caused me to keep quiet. I gave Mrs Forrester my word, and that is my bond. I dare not yield to the temptation to go blabbing— it already has been decided."

We soon reached our destination and entered our building. I ascended the stairs ahead of Holmes, who stayed behind to check with our landlady, Mrs Hudson, to see if anyone had left a message for him. When I went into our rooms, there was a crackling fire on the grate and, spookily, the silhouetted figure of a small human in an armchair near the hearth. I hurriedly lit an oil lamp to better view the person, who spoke not a word until I demanded to know who the intruder could be.

"I have come for help from Mr Sherlock Holmes," said the elderly, stoop-shouldered woman, whose ashen face was marked by deep wrinkles and whose thinning, snow-white hair was tucked partially under a plain black babushka.

"I am not he—I am his roommate and confidant, Dr Watson," I informed her. "Mr Holmes will be here directly." I asked how she got in, and our visitor confessed that she used the back door and came into our quarters through the ground-floor kitchen, then up to the first floor, where the unlocked door bore our address.

"I was chilly, so I built a fire to warm my bones and wait for the famous detective to get home," she stated with a distinctly foreign accent. "My name is Anna Barlova Pavlovna and I am from the Russian immigrant neighborhood in the East End of London. I am a widow in desperate need of an ally."

At that moment, Holmes appeared in the doorway, surprised to glimpse an aged female sitting in his preferred chair at that hour. "Mrs Hudson mentioned nothing about our having a guest. What is this all about, madam?" Holmes queried.

She repeated her name and situation, explaining that she had traveled to our suite under the cover of a foggy night because she was fearful that she might have been under surveillance where she lived.

"Are you afraid of the police?" Holmes wanted to learn.

"Yes, but not the local police—the *Okhrana*, the secret police in my motherland," she revealed. "They rely on torture and mayhem to extract information from the innocent, and they commit atrocities in plots against their adversaries."

"Perhaps you should tell me your whole story, from the very start," Holmes encouraged the fidgety lady, taking up the armchair next to hers.

"I shall be pleased to do that, sir, if in the end you will consider assisting me in my mission," Anna Pavlovna began, tugging on the sleeve of her navy-blue wool sweater and repositioning to her lap the large, brown envelope she cradled under her arm. "I was born in 1839 to parents who were serfs in Saint Petersburg, house servants to an aristocrat and treated with dignity. When Tsar Alexander II freed the serfs by decree in 1861, my family remained with the nobleman because he was so kind to us.

"One evening at a party in the household, I served sherry to the son of another aristocrat and he was attracted to me, as I was to him. I was a beautiful young woman then, and the young man very handsome. We arranged to meet at an inn for supper the next day, and later that week at a park, soon falling in love.

"He proposed marriage and I accepted, but news of our courtship presented a terrible shock to his mother and father, first because I was a Jew, and second because of my station in life. They disowned their only child and caused him to live in poverty as an apprentice to a cabinetmaker out in the countryside. He and I were wed a month later by a rabbi who took pity on us. Although we struggled to survive, we had many happy years together, until the Tsar was assassinated in 1881. His successor, Alexander III, reversed most of the progressive policies of his father and became a tyrant. My husband and I joined the revolutionary underground and were targeted for arrest by the Emperor's *Okhrana*. We fled to Lithuania, and then to England, where we remained in exile under the surname of Buk until my beloved husband, Mikhail, was murdered in his cabinet shop six days ago.

"I am afraid I am next, Mr Holmes, because of the activity in which my late husband and I were engaged since our flight to this country. I am a writer of novels in my native language, political allegories that inspire the social democrats in Russia. I smuggle the manuscripts through couriers to a printer in Saint Petersburg, who is also part of the underground, and he publishes the books for distribution to our comrades throughout the Empire. I have one of those manuscripts with me tonight, and in it is the fact that the wrong men were hanged for throwing the bomb that destroyed Tsar Alexander II. It was not conspirators from the People's Will who carried out the assassination, but rather henchmen of the nobility displeased with the Tsar's liberal decrees. I am to rendezvous with one of my couriers after I leave you. But the East End is teeming with spies and double-agents for the *Okhrana* and I believe they have identified me as the author of the banned books. My husband was a financial supporter of the revolution, and I suspect that is why he was killed—his throat was slashed from ear to ear—not simply because he was the victim of a robbery, as Scotland Yard presumed. My husband's safe was rifled when I found him, which is what led Inspector Hopkins to conclude that a bandit had done away with him. The culprit was looking for a manuscript, not money. My little house behind my husband's shop was also torn apart while I was away at the market.

"I told Inspector Hopkins all about my husband's involvement in the movement, but it amounted to nothing worth pursuing in the youthful policeman's eyes. He said the *Okhrana* could not operate in London without Scotland Yard being aware of it, and the intelligence unit never reported the existence of any such organization."

"I once had high hopes for Stanley Hopkins," Holmes interjected, "yet the more I hear of his methods the less impressed I am with his results. Now tell me, Mrs Pavlovna, what would you have me do to assist you?"

"You can avenge my impending death and expose the elements of the *Okhrana* so that my countrymen will know even more of the regime's evils," Mrs Pavlovna bravely predicted. "The more the people know of the truth, the more likely the overthrow of the brutal autocrat, Alexander Alexandrovich Romanov."

"Come now, Mrs Pavlovna, you must not consider your fate in such dire terms," Holmes pleaded. "The danger you face might only be the theft of a manuscript, not the end of your life. Possibly your husband resisted the intruder, and that is why he died."

"The *Okhrana* wish to silence me," she responded. "And the only means they have is to eliminate me. Otherwise, I shall continue creating my tales until I am too feeble to put pen to paper."

Holmes told her he would honour her request, then offered to accompany her safely home, to which she replied that doing so would only prolong the inevitable. "Besides," she added, "my courier would disappear without the manuscript if he saw someone he didn't recognise escorting me."

I suggested a hot cup of tea to the courageous old Russian woman before she ventured into the concealment of the darkness outside, but she declined the invitation and bade us farewell. "I appreciate your hospitality, but I am already late for the appointment with my contact," she said apologetically, then ambled down the stairs toward the rear exit, passing Mrs Hudson's rooms unnoticed.

"I can't imagine a more dedicated, loyal, and stoic individual," Holmes observed after she had departed. "What do you suppose of her chances of staying alive until morning, Watson?"

"She is no doubt crafty, slipping in and out of here like a ghost, so I assume she can manage to outwit a squad of secret police and their agents," I answered. "But what if they actually have

discovered that Anna Buk is Anna Barlova Pavlovna, the origina-
tor of subversive novels?"

"In that case," Holmes conjectured, "Inspector Hopkins could
have two coincidental homicides to probe that he attributes to the
work of a street thug."

Holmes excused himself and went up to his bedroom, coming
down a few moments later in his lavender dressing gown and re-
laxing near the fire with his Index, an encyclopedia he maintained
with memoranda on the world of crime, plus various other topics.

"It says in here that the *Okhrana* has far-flung tentacles," he
apprised me. "Its influence extends to other continents, including
Europe and America. So, it is altogether possible that Mrs Pavlovna's fear is justified."

Shortly after dawn the following day, Holmes shook me awake
from a peaceful sleep and curled his bony finger to summon me out
of bed. "Come, Watson, if you are wanting for another adventure
to chronicle," he beckoned. "I am anxious to determine if Mrs Pavlovna made it back to her little house last night without incident.
We can eat a quick breakfast at the Lime Street Cafe en route to
Aldgate Station."

Soon we were aboard an eastbound train to Craven Street in the
heart of the Russian immigrant community. Holmes, who studied
under a tutor in preparation for his trip to Odessa in the Tripoff
murder case, spoke a Ukrainian dialect when he sought directions
to the Buk cabinet shop from a vendor selling apples from a cart.
It was a long, depressing walk, past hundreds of sheds and shan-
ties and tenements. In these hovels, the population congregated at
sunset after eking out a pittance, day after grueling day, hawking
food or toiling at trades that produced wares only the well-to-do
from other sections of the city could afford to buy.

In better than average condition, the Pavlovna domicile was set
apart from the late husband's shop by a short gravel path that ended at the intricately carved front door, apparently the handiwork
of the cabinetmaker. Mrs Pavlovna, whom we saw peeking out
the kitchen window from behind the lace curtains, responded to
Holmes's knock quickly and greeted us somberly. "I am in a melancholy mood today, missing my Mikhail terribly," she explained,
and politely invited us inside. "You are here to solve his murder?"

"That is one reason," Holmes replied, and then said he was curious to know if the manuscript was on its way to Saint Petersburg.

"Yes, it is in the proper hands, and God will see that it gets to the printer in due course," she told him, the conversation now lifting her dampened spirits a bit.

"No one tried to harm you yet?" Holmes continued.

"Not yet, but I am still wary—and you, Mr Holmes, must be cautious asking questions, because the enemy of the people has big ears," Mrs Pavlovna warned.

"I am always careful," Holmes went on, "so you needn't worry about me. Tell me, on the day your husband was killed, did you notice anything out of the ordinary?"

"I did," she disclosed matter-of-factly. "Two men, strangers in the neighborhood, were sitting on a bench across the street from my husband's shop when I went to the market. When I got back, they were gone, nowhere in sight."

"Did you tell this to Inspector Hopkins?" Holmes queried.

"He never asked, and I was so grief-stricken at the time I didn't think to mention it to him. I don't believe he is very thorough. Or maybe the violent death of a poor man from the slums is not so important to Scotland Yard," she blurted, covering her mouth with the palm of her right hand and widening her dark eyes.

"What did these two men look like? Describe each of them, and what they were wearing," Holmes prodded.

"One had long legs, the other short," Mrs Pavlovna advised. "They were not talking; they were just watching. The one with long legs was about thirty years old and had a tan coat with knickerbockers, along with a cloth cap pulled down over the bridge of his long nose. The other man was about fifty years old and had a brown waistcoat, and wore laced brown boots. He wore a derby, and he had frizzy grey hair. And he had spectacles with thick lenses."

"Excellent, my dear!" Holmes exclaimed, and he praised her observational ability, charming her in the special way he had with women. "Is there anything else about these men that you can remember?"

"Only that the one with long legs was smoking a cigarette with a cork tip," she added.

"You have been more than helpful," he told her. "Try to get some rest—I can see by the shaded circles under your eyes that you haven't been sleeping."

"It is hard without my Mikhail by my side. I pray that I live long enough for time to heal me," she answered.

Holmes and I left Mrs Pavlovna in a better frame of mind than when we arrived. Before we started out on our return journey, however, Holmes let himself in the unlocked cabinet shop and spent about fifteen minutes examining the scene of the crime, while I sat on the bench across the street and puffed on my clay pipe. I could see every move Holmes made inside through the two large front windows. It was a perfect vantage point if I wanted to be certain the occupant of the shop was alone.

"There wasn't any sign of a scuffle, Watson," Holmes related when he emerged and joined me on the bench for a smoke. "That could only mean there were two intruders, one, the stronger of the pair who would have immobilised the old man, and another who cut his throat."

"It is probable, then, that the attackers came here with murderous intent," I volunteered, "because a routine robbery would likely be carried out by a single assailant."

"That is a workable theory, but we must have even more data than what I already have gathered, else we jump to the wrong conclusion," Holmes chided.

"But if what I surmise is correct," I persisted, "then Mrs Pavlovna's suspicions about the *Okhrana* agents might be true."

"It is surely worth considering, Watson," Holmes intoned. "Now let's make our next stop the headquarters of Scotland Yard to determine whether the intransigent Stanley Hopkins has made any progress in his line of inquiry."

We alighted from the train at Whitehall Place and, in no time at all, we were waiting in a vacant office of the Metropolitan Police Service for Inspector Hopkins to finish interviewing a witness to a different event altogether.

"I am swamped with a number of investigations all at once," he said as he poked his head in the door and scurried down the hallway. When he returned a few moments later, he begged our pardon for his inattentiveness to our concerns. "I have never seen it so busy," he complained, adding that current circumstances were sufficiently cooled down to allow him to devote some time to our problem.

Holmes empathised and quickly got to the point, to which Inspector Hopkins reacted with chagrin. "Your purpose puzzles me," he said. "Why would you be interested in a simple robbery in an impoverished part of town when you have all those high-profile cases I've been reading about in Dr Watson's magazine articles?"

"Not all my affairs warrant extensive publicity, Inspector, as Watson can attest," Holmes countered. "In this instance, I am engaged to protect the widow, Mrs Buk, because she is anticipating that something dreadful could be attempted against her."

"Oh, balderdash," Inspector Hopkins sputtered. "All this nonsense about cloak-and-dagger enforcers of the Emperor in Russia is the product of a wild imagination. I am inclined to speculate that one of our home-grown hoodlums is responsible for what happened to her husband, which is why I have my informants pounding the cobblestones to unearth a more practical outcome."

"But if it was a simple robbery, as you hypothesise, what cash or valuables could the thief have been after? The victim was a person of less than modest means," Holmes challenged.

"These immigrants horde money like a squirrel hordes acorns in autumn, and the bandits know that all too well. Mr Buk had a safe, didn't he? Something of value must have been kept in it," the official detective contended finally.

We wished Inspector Hopkins well in his endeavours and rode in a cab back to our rooms at Baker Street, marveling at his closed mind.

When we entered our flat, Holmes tossed his cape and jacket onto the coat rack, then rolled up his shirt sleeves before he sat at the deal-topped table and ignited the Bunsen burner. "I took a sample of dried blood from a pool on the floor of the cabinet shop, and I shall analyse it, for I am convinced both killers were spattered with it. They will have the deceased's blood on their clothing when we encounter them," he postulated.

While Holmes was occupied with his vials and chemistry, I made notes of the developments thus far, activities which brought us to the dinner hour. I offered to pick up sandwiches at the corner shop and Holmes readily concurred. "I am not hungry enough for a full meal," he said off-handedly, "and sandwiches will be faster. We need to be going soon. There is no time to waste."

"Going? Where?" I wanted to know.

"To Claridge's Hotel in the East End near the Russian immigrant community," he apprised me.

"What do you expect to find there?" I insisted on learning.

"Our two suspects!" he barked, saying not a further word.

The adventure would prove to be harrowing, taking us to within centimeters of losing our lives.

It was nearly nightfall when Holmes and I briskly navigated curvy Curzon Street, where Claridge's Hotel stood with its five stories facing the intersection of Mincing Lane, a seldom-used avenue that paralleled the main road into the Russian section of the city. We went through the dim, shabby lobby to the hotel desk clerk's station, which was unoccupied. Holmes pulled the bell rope and we heard it ring in a room behind the counter. More than a minute passed before a raggedly-dressed, middle-aged man with crumbs dangling from his black, bushy mustache opened the door to the back room and growled at us. "Seven shillings for each of you, if you share the bed," he asserted.

Holmes dug in his trouser pocket and came up with the right amount, dropped it on the desk, and then showed the clerk a sovereign. "This is for you if you can tell us where we can find our two friends," he said, almost whispering. He described the men Mrs Pavlovna saw on the bench.

"Number 33," came the rapid response, and with that the clerk swept his hand across the counter and snatched the money from Holmes's fingers, glancing around the lobby to see if any of the four men lingering there had noticed the transaction.

"We would like a room close to Number 33," Holmes requested. Our cooperative host answered that the one across the hall was vacant, Number 32. "Go on up then—no key, there are no locks," he snapped. Nor was there a register to sign, which disappointed Holmes, because he wanted to establish the identities of the two suspects. We climbed the steps and entered Number 32 after Holmes listened with his ear against the door of Number 33.

"No one seems to be in there, Watson, so you stand guard in the hallway and signal me if you hear footsteps coming," Holmes ordered as we shed our outer garments and threw them on the squeaky bed.

"It makes me nervous when you trespass, but I'll position myself at the top of the stairs and rap twice on the door if I detect any sound of someone approaching," I informed him.

Holmes crossed the gloomy corridor and stealthily went into the opposite room, but he almost instantly came out and waved for me to return to Number 32.

"One of them, the tall one, is asleep and there was no indication of where the other could be," he announced quietly when we were safely out of sight. "I was in there long enough, however, to find a pack of Red Kamel cigarettes next to the basin on the wash stand."

"What does that mean?" I asked.

"It is the same brand as the crushed butt I discovered on the floor of the cabinet shop," Holmes disclosed. "It is unavailable as an import here, and it is made from an expensive Turkish blend of tobacco with a cork tip. It is much preferred by the elite in Russia. Commoners can't pay the price."

"So we are on the right track—the smoker must have come from Russia recently, and he was inside the cabinet shop," I observed.

"A brilliant and plausible deduction, Watson," Holmes commended.

We left our door slightly ajar and waited in the unlit room for almost three hours before we heard movement near Number 33. Holmes watched through the opening as the short, bespectacled hotel guest went into Number 33 carrying a large, brown envelope the size of the one Mrs Pavlovna brought with her to Baker Street the preceding night.

"He has the manuscript," Holmes whispered to me. "Mrs Pavlovna's courier, or the one next in line, apparently is in league with this pair. Otherwise, if there was a chance of a fight before the contact was relieved of the package, not one but both operatives would have gone to intercept it."

"What do we do now?" I asked.

"We wait even longer, and if they leave the room together, we shall follow them, for I believe if anything is about to happen to Mrs Pavlovna, tonight is the time."

There was no activity at Number 33 as the midnight hour came and went. While we were idle, I wondered to Holmes how he knew to come to Claridge's Hotel.

"On the floor of the cabinet shop was an empty box of wooden matches with the name of this place on the top," he revealed. "I deduced that no one other than the killer or his accomplice could have discarded the box, because there was no scent of cigarette smoke in the Pavlovna household, meaning the husband didn't indulge. The presence of the match box and the cigarette butt told me even more, though. The assailants spent more than enough time with their victim than was necessary to take his life. They obviously were interrogating him for a lengthy period, probably trying to coerce him into confessing that his wife was the writer in exile, and to reveal to them the location of her latest work. Terrified though he must have been, he never compromised her with information they were searching to gain. That is the reason they rifled his safe." But Holmes said he needed more evidence than what he already had before reporting his findings to Scotland Yard. "Something more convincing to Inspector Hopkins to demonstrate he has been barking up the wrong tree," Sherlock Holmes concluded.

I was dozing in a chair at about two o'clock in the morning when Holmes placed his fingertips over my lips and roused me. "I detected some activity across the hallway, so be prepared to move out, Watson," he said in a hushed tone.

It wasn't long before both occupants of Number 33 left the room and started down the stairs. We gave them about a half-minute head start while we donned our jackets and capes, then walked on tip-toes to the steps. We quietly went down, pausing before we reached the lobby until we heard the door to the outside close. Holmes and I both were armed, our .32 caliber revolvers loaded and secured in our right-hand jacket pockets. We trailed our two subjects at a moderately fast pace down Mincing Lane toward the vicinity of Mrs Pavlovna's house. Holmes led the way, I at his heels. He ducked behind a tree now and then in case the two men looked back to see if they were followed. Once, they halted, as if to orient themselves, and turned in our direction, but we were hidden behind the corner of an apartment building.

The men walked abreast with determination, finally turning onto Rochester Row, on which Mrs Pavlovna's dwelling was located a couple of blocks farther up.

As we turned the corner, we came face-to-face with two other men, each brandishing a handgun pointing directly at us. They menaced us briefly until one of them spoke in Russian, so only Holmes could understand what the assailant was saying.

"They want us to accompany them to that shed and go inside, Watson," Holmes told me, nodding toward a tiny, dilapidated structure to the rear of a butcher shop. We complied. Inside was a bare table and four chairs, plus two cots. The more aggressive of the two motioned for us to sit, so we did as he indicated. Thoughts of our losing precious time to rescue Mrs Pavlovna raced through my brain, and I was certain of the same occurring in Holmes's mind. Neither of the hostage-takers spoke again for several moments, until the one giving the orders glared at Holmes and demanded to know if we were the official police.

Holmes told him no, but offered nothing more. It seemed to make the man angry and he sat down at the table with his weapon trained between Holmes's eyes. Holmes slipped his left hand under the tabletop and casually dipped his right hand into his jacket pocket. With one motion, he heaved the table upward, knocking both men backwards and off balance. They fired rapid bursts in succession, indiscriminately, and missed us entirely. At the same instant Holmes squeezed off all of his five shots through his clothing and struck both men once, each squarely in the chest, killing the interrogator before he folded onto the dirt floor, and mortally wounding his partner.

Holmes leaned over the man who was still conscious, but barely. "*Okhrana*?" Holmes bellowed.

"Da," the man gasped, and died.

"Quickly, Watson!" Holmes yelled. "To the old woman's house!"

Holmes was peering through the bedroom window when I caught up with him, breathing hard. Mrs Pavlovna, flat on her back, was bound to the bed posts with babushkas around her wrists, and the suspect wearing spectacles stood at her side, clutching a straight razor. His accomplice was seated next to the headboard, smoking a cigarette. There was talking, but we could discern nothing.

Holmes crept to the open front door and entered the kitchen. I removed the revolver from my pocket and lagged quietly and closely behind him.

"They won't realise my pistol is empty, so we shall both rush in on them at the same time with our weapons flashing," he whispered.

We filled the bedroom doorway side-by-side and ambushed the assailants, startling them sufficiently to cause them to freeze. Holmes ordered the short one to drop the razor, but instead he thrust it to Mrs Pavlovna's throat.

"Drop guns or I kill her," he threatened in broken English.

"Hurt her and you are a dead man," Holmes warned.

"He is a dead man nonetheless," I added, taking aim and shooting. My bullet creased the reprobate's skull, sending his derby flying and him hurtling across the room, shrieking and bleeding profusely. He cowered in a corner, holding his crimson forehead, weeping and begging for mercy. I had an urge to finish him off, but resisted it. Holmes grabbed the razor from the oval rug and began to free Mrs Pavlovna while I covered the two criminals, the muzzle of my revolver alternating between them. The one in the chair spoke broken English as well, adamantly proclaiming it was not his idea to murder the Pavlovnas, as if that mattered.

"They were trying to get me to name all my cohorts in the movement, and give up the locations of their homes," Mrs Pavlovna said forcefully. "The tall one said I would join my husband tonight if I didn't cooperate, but the *Okhrana* don't know I am a true patriot with a stubborn streak stronger than their devotion to the dictator."

"Hand me your revolver, Watson," Holmes instructed, "and see if you can roust that constable sleeping on the bench across the street. If all the commotion in here didn't awaken him, it is possible he is among the dearly departed."

I left, Holmes keeping the miscreants at bay with four cartridges in the cylinder. On the way out, I hurriedly examined the wounded man's injury and handed him my handkerchief, advising him to apply pressure to his gushing scalp. I returned about five minutes later with the drowsy policeman, to whom Holmes provided only sketchy details of what had transpired. Befuddled, the official stepped outside and blew his whistle to summon help.

When two more constables came in with him, Holmes introduced us to them, along with criminals Leonid Gutnik and Vladimir Prost: "These two gentlemen are purported to be agents of the *Okhrana*, the secret police in Russia. Mr Gutnik has admitted they murdered Mrs Buk's husband last week, and they still carry the bloodstains on their coats. They were on the verge of killing Mrs Buk tonight until Dr Watson and I disrupted their devious plans. Inspector Hopkins is investigating the murder of Mr Buk. Please arrange for the inspector to meet us here as soon as he can."

"We'll bring him in his nightshirt if we must, Mr Holmes," said one of the constables, a sergeant. "I've read about you in the periodicals, you know, and two things are certain—you always get your man, and what you say is gospel."

"I'm pleased you believe that," Holmes replied, "for there is something else I'm compelled to tell you now. There are two dead bodies in the shed attached to the butcher shop up the street. I shot them while they held Dr Watson and me at gunpoint to prevent us from saving the life of Mrs Buk. They definitely were agents of the secret police, a fact one of them confirmed before he expired. I'm sure Inspector Hopkins will have no difficulty ironing all this out before it becomes an international incident."

"Two corpses, eh? Inspector Hopkins will have a full day ahead of him," remarked the sergeant. "I'd better see to it that he gets an early start. I'll leave one of my officers here with you to help guard the prisoners."

After the sergeant had gone off to fulfill his duties, Holmes questioned the taller, younger of the two culprits about how they came into possession of Mrs Pavlovna's manuscript.

"From a party loyal to Tsar," he related, but refused to name their confederate. "I wish to stay England, like him; death for me if I go back Russia after failing mission."

"Death awaits you here, too, on the gallows," Holmes stated grimly.

It was almost sunrise when Inspector Hopkins arrived to sort out the events with a humbled attitude and an open mind. "I don't know yet how to express these circumstances to the reporters without embarrassing the Yard," he lamented as the assassins were escorted away in shackles.

Holmes and I returned to the hotel to retrieve Mrs Pavlovna's manuscript from room Number 33 and, later, delivered it to her. It came as no shock to the old woman that one of her couriers was part of the *Okhrana* network.

"I have always been suspicious about one of them, Anatoly Breznikop, because his roots are in the aristocracy and he can travel to and from Russia without interference," she said. As we conversed, she sliced us each an ample portion of rhubarb pie that she said she had baked the afternoon before. "I bake every day, but not today—I am still too nervous about what has happened," she allowed.

"Place your trust only in those who have earned it, my sweet lady, and always make a carbon copy of your manuscripts to send through other channels, just in case the originals fall into the hands of a traitor," Holmes recommended to her while we ate our treat.

And thus ended the affair of the old Russian woman, but for this epilogue:

About a month had gone by without mention of her when Holmes called my attention to an item in the *Evening Standard* about the unexpected death of one Anatoly Breznikop, which appeared to be the result of a heart attack until relatives demanded an autopsy.

"It says here that Scotland Yard regards it as a homicide, Holmes," I commented, "because the autopsy revealed an overdose of codeine in his bloodstream. Do you intend to involve yourself in the matter?"

"So far, only to the point where we should visit Mrs Pavlovna and find out what she knows of it," he informed me.

The following afternoon, we were seated at her kitchen table watching her dish up pieces of warm apple pie that she earlier had placed on the window sill to cool.

"Anatoly sent me a message the day before he died," she recalled, "and said he would stop by on the morrow in the event I had a new book prepared. He lied to me then, insisting that two men accosted him and stole my manuscript, though he bravely tried to fend them off. He ate pie and drank coffee, then went on his way. He reached Lark Hall Lane, just a short distance away, and collapsed, grasping at his chest. That is all I know."

She gave us a half smile.

"Eat up, men. Yours is not poisoned like the pies I feed to the rats," she assured us.

LONDON 1890

Mackenzie Clarkes

Horse hooves,
Pounding,
The streets,
Tires,
Splashing,
On curbs,
Hansom cabs
And rolling,
Through fog
At night.

JUGGLING WITH SHERLOCK'S FRIEND

by Mark Levy, BSI

Sherlock Holmes, Dr John Watson, and I were doing whisky shots with Guinness beer chasers at *Moriarty's Tavern,* a cool, but still damp bar on Second Avenue in Manhattan in the middle of a hot weekday afternoon. Actually, Watson was out-drinking his friend and me.

The bar was one of my favorites, big enough to have six beers on tap and every kind of booze known to man, while retaining its neighborhood flavor. It included an adult floor show that began when the joint opened every day at noon. It was 3:00 p.m. when the two Victorian dudes appeared and *Moriarty's* was already half full. Executives can lack the patience to wait for happy hour to get a buzz.

I still don't completely understand how Watson and Holmes got to my favorite New York bar a hundred years after they had retired, but here they were, solid as Mazarin stones, beryl coronets, or blue carbuncles. Watson wore a thick, Victorian hound's-tooth suit and carried a walking cane and a crocodile doctor's bag. Holmes wore, well, what Holmes wears when he's not in disguise.

The great detective wrapped his slender fingers around his beer glass, attempting to warm it.

"Cellar temperature of about 50° F., Watson," Holmes said. "As you know, it's the civilized way to drink Guinness."

But I noticed the cooler temperature of the brewski didn't seem to slow old Dr Watson down at all.

"An extraordinary pub," Holmes said, studying the neon lighting and overhead electric fan. "The colonies are quite advanced now."

He pulled out a pipe from his inverness and began to fill it with tobacco.

"Sorry, Mr Holmes," I said. "No smoking is permitted in here."

Holmes looked perturbed. "I withdraw my laudable observation about this establishment," he said. "More restrictive laws then we are accustomed to. One would have thought it impossible for a society to be more restrictive than our own. Curious."

"Yeah," I said. "The Surgeon General has taken the fun out of a lot of things, but we still have sex, drugs, and rock 'n' roll."

"Are you all ruled by military men?"

"No, but the Surgeon General is the head of the Pubic Health Service. And it's not a man, by the way. I recently Googled her. She's a medical doctor, an African-American woman named Regina Benjamin."

Both Holmes and Watson were dumbfounded. Watson actually sputtered his beer back into his glass. Holmes recovered his composure first. "Do you mean to say a girl, and an African one at that, forbids you Yanks to smoke? That is most astonishing."

"Surely you must be mistaken, sir," Watson said. "The gentler sex would hardly survive the rigors of a medical education or be exposed to the less savory aspects of the human body, especially beneath the skin. And in any event, she would be unwelcome to practice at hospital."

"Under the circumstances, gentlemen, it might be best not to tell you about the President of the United States."

Just then the lights dimmed and a surgically-enhanced, well-endowed exotic dancer walked out onto the bar before us, wearing nothing but her stiletto heels and cheap toilet water. She executed a slow motion split directly in front of Watson.

I thought the old doc was going to have a cardiac arrest. He held his breath for thirty seconds and his eyes just about popped out of his head. His face turned from pasty white to red to blue.

Holmes observed that the young, top-heavy girl bit her fingernails, that she had been pregnant at least once, that she cared for a very young child and an aging, white-haired woman, that she had recently removed a wedding ring, and that her natural hair color was darker than the hairpiece she wore. With all modesty, I should mention that I could have made that last observation myself. But who, I ask you, would notice fingernails on a stripper?

While my new acquaintances were absorbing Miss Anti-Gravity Mammaries' performance and digesting the shocking information about women physicians, I thought it best to change the subject.

"What brings you so far in time and geography?" I asked.

"A curious structure that appears to have been produced in your time, not ours."

Holmes reached into his pocket and withdrew a flat, black article the size of a thumbnail. Along one side, a number of parallel metallic lines extended to the periphery. On the flat surface appeared the characters

© **2013.**

"I believe your technology may be sufficiently advanced to handle this piece that I discovered with the possessions of one Arthur Cadogan West. My friend has chronicled the case under the title, 'The Adventure of the Bruce-Partington Plans.'"

Holmes fingered the piece in his hand. "This object may be related to secret plans in connection with a highly advanced marine vessel. Indeed, the technology used in that vessel was suspiciously more advanced than anything created up to that time. The origin of aspects of the vessel was unknown, but experts believe the concepts could not have been developed by the individuals known in the case. Do you have an idea as to the function of this small article? It is quite inflexible and I cannot open it without destroying it. A remarkable material. Those numbers appear to be your year, 2013, which led us to travel here."

"Looks like a plastic memory card," I said. "You don't know about plastics, but I know a dude who can probably read this."

"Read it?" Holmes asked.

"Yeah. It could have documents and maybe drawings or video stored in it."

"I hardly think even a single sheet of paper could be folded so small as to fit in a container this thin."

"Right you are, Sherlock." I couldn't resist smiling as those words came out. "Information is stored by a computer, which is too complicated to get into with you. All you need to know is it's coded, electrically coded."

Watson stirred from his reverie when he heard those words.

"Indeed," he said in a condescending way, "we are able to analyze the most elaborate codes. Recently, for example, we had occasion to decipher a string of stick figures that represented letters. The figures appeared to dance, but…"

"Not really the same thing," I interrupted, hoping to be as dismissive as he was boastful. "If you give me the card, I'll ask my guy if he can print the contents, okay?"

"How long will this procedure take?" Holmes asked.

"My guy is just two blocks away. I'll take it to him now and let you know what he says."

Although Holmes was reluctant to let the card leave his sight, Watson convinced him to give it to me.

"The origin and many details of a very advanced submarine may be on what you call that card," Holmes said. "It appears to have been created, somehow, many years after the incident with which we were involved. You say it is impossible to reveal the truth without the computer device. If I've said it once, I've said it a hundred times: once the impossible has been eliminated…"

This time it was Watson's turn to interrupt. "Not again, Holmes. You *have* said it a hundred times, and I've heard it at least that many."

Holmes gave Watson a withering look, but then continued. "How that card was transported back in time to London may forever be a mystery."

Holmes searched my eyes for a few seconds, as if to see if I could be trusted. I must have passed the test. Holmes chuckled and handed the memory card to me. I took off to see Dave, my computer buddy. He had some time available to check it out and told me to return in two hours with ten bucks.

By the time I returned to the bar, a new exotic dancer had replaced the first one. Watson was equally enthralled. Holmes was still preoccupied with his surroundings.

As the afternoon went on, we talked about crime and violence in the city. Watson mentioned Holmes's expertise with singlesticks, whatever they are. I don't know why he mentioned singlesticks in the first place. It was just after Holmes mumbled something about applying a space-time Lorentz derivative function of the binomial theory to travel through a trans-temporal inflection point.

"The calculation is a simple one," Holmes said. Now it was Holmes who was being condescending. What was with those British guys?

"Nevertheless," Watson said, "the trip was extremely unsettling to my stomach. I resolve to concentrate on armchair consulting from now on." He hesitated and glanced around. "With the assistance of my friend, Mr Holmes, of course. Frankly, in my stories I gave him more sole credit for our joint observations than he actually deserves. It makes for better character development, according to my literary agent."

Not to be outdone by Holmes, singlestick-wise, I told Watson I was a fairly aggressive amateur juggler myself.

"No special physical conditioning is required to juggle, just an ability to move your arms and close your hands."

Watson was visibly pleased with this news. His eyes opened wide and a smile formed under his mustache.

"Indeed," he exclaimed, "I am not without a certain athletic dexterity, having played rugby for the Blackheath Football Club."

"Neuromuscular facilitation, doctor," I muttered into my beer glass.

"Might you elucidate, old chap?"

Watson moved his eyes down the dancer's body and focused on her upper thighs.

"Muscle memory," I said, watching the stripper and noticing I was getting aroused in spite of myself. "Can't learn to juggle abstractly. No three-pipe armchair cogitation for this one, my learned friend. You've got to practice, practice, practice until your hands know where to go. It's automatic, without thinking…like a concert pianist, you know? Just feel the balls, anticipate where they'll be, without keeping track of each one in motion."

Watson nodded, continuing to absorb the sight, sound, and smell of the stripper.

"I say," he said, turning in her direction. "We really should encourage this sort of exercise in England, Holmes. I am tempted to write a paper of advantages and submitting it to the *Royal Medical Society Journal*."

"Are you referring to juggling or to the young lady in front of us?" I asked.

Understandably distracted, Watson didn't answer my question. He said, "Yes, yes. Quite. Indeed."

"My mind is like a racing engine," Holmes said. "Engaging in a purely physical, mindless activity such as juggling does not require ratiocination, so it holds no allure for me."

I turned my attention again to Watson, for whom the stripper obviously did provide sufficient allure.

"Some people are natural jugglers," I said. "It's best to start with an odd number of balls."

"Holmes," Watson said, "shall we give it a go?"

Holmes seemed resigned. "Surely you jest, Watson. Blackheath was years ago. But if you insist on embarrassing yourself publicly in a foreign country, I shall be happy to observe from a distance."

I dropped a sawbuck on the bar for the dancer and studiously avoided eye contact. Watson placed a shiny British coin next to my offering and reached out to pat her ankle, a cross between an avuncular and a perverted gesture.

"Hey, watch it, Grandpa," she said. "Hands off the merchandise."

On the way out of the bar, Watson told me he was sure he could attract women if he could do something exotic and unusual…such as juggling; and he wanted *me* to teach him. I told him no. He said he'd make it worth my while. He said he knew what it takes to pick up girls. You had to have a gimmick. A doctor's bag and a British accent were good, but balls in the air were better.

I told him my gimmick was not moving anything but my drinking elbow for hours on end. And I also shared with him my desire *not* to meet another woman—not ever again—after my recent four-year fiasco called a marriage with a barracuda named Mary.

At the mention of her name, Watson grew misty-eyed. But Watson, he can be one persistent cuss and he really, *really,* wanted to meet American women.

"I have enjoyed the company of young ladies in three separate continents," he confided, "but not yet in New York City."

I have to admit I admire a person who reaches his goal unless, of course, his goal is to force me to have one, too.

"I must implore you to teach me to juggle," Watson said, pulling me by the arm, either to propel me to the door or to steady himself. And so, despite my slurred, inarticulate protests, we walked—staggered, really—out of the bar and into bright sunlight. Watson leaned heavily on his walking stick.

"Have you fellows remembered to take along sunglasses?" I asked, as I fished for my shades.

"I prefer not to wear smoked glasses, what you call sunglasses," Holmes said, inspecting my glasses before I could find my ears. "They may obscure the very details I find it important to observe."

"These designer glasses are polarized," I said. "Very expensive."

"Do they contain precious metals or jewels?" he asked.

"No. They're cheap plastic and expensive glass."

"Plastic—similar to the memory card?"

"Exactly, sort of. It's material that became popular after the Second World War. Oops. Guess you wouldn't know about that, either. We can save that discussion for another day."

Arm in arm, like two fat old English women strolling on the banks of the Thames, Watson and I moved downtown past 55th Street on Second Avenue as rush hour began. Holmes followed a few steps behind.

"I am quite impressed with the revealing clothing your ladies wear," Watson said.

"When they wear clothing at all, you mean."

Holmes interrupted our intellectual conversation. "Mind these motorcars," he said. "They appear to be unforgiving metal."

"And plastic," I added, smiling.

We found a novelty shop crammed to the ceiling with cheapjack items: plastic toy handcuffs, bubble gum cigars, magic card tricks, and balls, a zillion balls, from the little, solid, rubber balls that kids use to play jacks, to huge, air-filled beach balls. We had hit New York's spheroidal jackpot. Holmes inspected one ball after another as if they held clues to the meaning of life.

I settled on old-fashioned, pink Spaldings, the size of tennis balls, a dozen for $25. We paid for them and, on the sidewalk, loaded them into Watson's doctor's bag. Then we headed for Rockefeller Plaza.

Here's some advice: Don't ever walk three streets down and two avenues over in Manhattan with a slightly inebriated, old-fashioned, horny doctor. He approached women with the subtlety of a bear in a honey-bottling plant, spewing obscure and ribald comments. Yet he mysteriously transmogrified himself into an irresistibly beguiling gentleman. At least he thought so.

Holmes wanted to observe, while Watson wanted to attract the attention of women whose libidos were the size of Piccadilly Circus. And he was convinced juggling was the means to that end.

"Now to impress some girls, old chap," he said as we staked out a corner of the plaza.

Watson began to remove balls from his doctor's bag. I suggested three of them was a good start. Our corner of the plaza was in the shade with no obstructions above us.

Rush hour can be profitable for street performers. If properly entertained, at least some passers-by will linger. For Watson—as indiscriminate a phylogynist as Holmes was distrustful of women—it was merely a numbers game. I never met an elderly gentleman who wanted to be laid so badly or who was so tenacious in executing a basically preposterous plan to do so.

"Okay, Watson, watch me, and then you try it. Two balls in one hand like this, one in the other."

I started off with the standard three-ball cascade for awhile and then executed a reachacross. Watson's eyes narrowed, but he stood absolutely still, transfixed like a three-year-old on the Fourth of July or whatever the equivalent is in merry Olde England.

Juggling, like bicycle riding, is easy to explain, but there's no substitute for experience. It can take months of effort to get the hang of it. In the beginning, the objects, called props, fly all over the place shooting out from the body at unexpected angles. When a juggler's hands move automatically, he knows he's arrived. It becomes as easy and subconscious as breathing. The student progresses from silk scarves, because they slowly float rather than fall, to bean bags, rubber balls, raw eggs, bowling balls, or chainsaws. And once the beginner can handle three props, he adds a couple more.

Watson took the props from me gently and, as God is my witness, without hesitating, he started juggling the three balls. He was an instant and perfect juggler. Didn't miss a beat. Didn't bobble even one ball. Most remarkable thing I've ever seen, short of the man himself appearing in the 21st century, affable and sleazy as a political candidate. He looked straight ahead, barely blinking, while his hands pumped rhythmically, releasing the balls as soon as he grasped them, progressing from cascades to fountains to showers. His performance was mesmerizing.

Most new jugglers start with one cycle and slowly work their way up to two. That alone can take weeks of practice. But not Watson. Like a ski racer who hasn't learned to stop, he performed so many back-to-back cycles I lost count. He wouldn't quit. His arms never got tired, even in that heavy, hot overcoat. It was as if he were born to juggle. If ever a person found his special talent, that day it was Watson. He may have been an excellent chronicler of the adventures of Sherlock Holmes, but he was an incredible juggler.

"Watson," Holmes said, as balls were tossed ever higher in the air. "Watson, I never get your limits."

"Elementary," Watson said with a wink in my direction. "A wise man once told me it is a capital mistake to underestimate the importance of observation and sometimes even criminal not to act on that knowledge."

He began to increase speed, tossing the balls into lower orbits. Soon the balls and his hands were a blur. His look of concentration was ferocious. After only a short time, Watson was already better than I was or could ever hope to be.

I threw two more balls at him rather forcefully, but he didn't miss a beat. He tossed the five balls accurately and effortlessly, as if he had been practicing since 1895; and then he really left me in the dust, taking on seven, nine, and finally eleven.

I had to remind myself to breathe.

Holmes settled himself, cross-legged, on the pavement, finally lighting his pipe. He observed people gawking in awe and delight at Watson and managed to identify three pickpockets and an undercover cop along the way. He noticed the types of women who responded to Watson's maneuvers. They tended to be brunettes, were of Victorian girth, and were shorter than average. I sensed him filing people and their characteristics away in his mind. I mentioned that to him.

"I place knowledge in my attic which might be useful," he said, "and make sure it is not jumbled up with a lot of other things. That way, I have no difficulty in laying my hands upon the important facts."

Meanwhile, balls shot out of Watson's hands like cannonballs, twenty feet into the air, two per second. He performed a pirouette, launched three between his legs—which I informed him is called an Albert—and bounced them off the ground, off the wall, and off his head, never blinking, never faltering, never dropping.

Holmes was as excited as the onlookers. He rose from his place on the sidewalk with one fluid motion and began to walk through the appreciative crowd collecting donations in the shopping bag that had held the Spaldings. We made almost 400 hundred bucks before a cop broke up the party.

I intended to return with my share of the profit directly to the secure comfort of the bar where it had all begun for a few more rounds before I passed out. I had retained my recent, post-divorce talent for getting blotto, thank goodness.

First I visited Dave, my computer guy again, who had down-loaded the contents of the memory card. He printed the text and drawings of a patent application for a submarine navigation and control system. The inventors were Fred Bruce and James Parting-ton. They worked for General Dynamics.

"Here you go, my friend," I said, returning to the bar and hand-ing Holmes the sheaf of papers and his memory card. "As I sus-pected, the computer had no problems with this. You owe me an Andy Jackson."

"Andy Jackson?"

"Twenty bucks. Oh, just buy me another round and we'll be even."

"This information is worth a good deal more than currency," Holmes said. "The security of England was at stake and the origin of the highly advanced submarine is now unveiled by 21st century technology. We arrived at the precise time and place to get the missing piece for our little puzzle."

Holmes was clearly satisfied with his day's achievement.

As for Watson, the greatest juggler who had ever lived, I never saw him again after he hooked up and disappeared that afternoon with two working girls.

As for me, I'm proud I taught John H Watson something. Many would probably consider juggling a useless skill, but who's to say it isn't as important as discovering a hidden tunnel or exposing a murderer or recovering plans for a modern submarine?

I'm sure Holmes would agree.

THE ADVENTURE OF THE WHITE PYTHON

by Adam McFarlane

While I sat for breakfast one summer morning, my wife Mary ushered my old friend Sherlock Holmes to our table.

"What an unprecedented surprise!" I exclaimed.

Holmes's disappointment over my marriage had resulted in an absence of nearly a year. Although Holmes was the reason that I first met and fell in love with Mary Morstan, for she came to him with a case I recounted in *A Sign of Four*, she wisely finished her breakfast alone in the drawing room. Sherlock Holmes had no interest in romance and distrusted women altogether.

The sun warmed the dining room. Blue and white china spread across the table linen, and pink roses reflected in the silver epergne.

Our maid Sally entered and laid out a knife, a fork, an egg cup, plates and glasses for Holmes. He poured himself a cup of coffee. He inhaled the smell through his hawk-like nose and he smiled, crinkling the corners of his grey eyes. His long fingers wrapped around the cup.

"Thank you, Watson. I've eaten nothing today, having just woken up with a telegram awaiting my reply."

Scraping a spot of char off the rashers, I asked, "What did the telegram say?"

"A pet shop's prized albino python disappeared, and the proprietor wants me to find it." Holmes encountered many animals in his cases, including a horse named Silver Blaze, the Giant Rat of Sumatra, and in my absence, the Lion's Mane jellyfish. A Christmas goose held the clue to the theft of the Blue Carbuncle, but never before had Holmes been called upon to find a missing pet.

I pushed cruets and the saltcellar closer to him. "After you've had your fill, we'll go straight-away."

With a raised a hand, he said, "I've already been there to meet the owner, Laszlo Lazar. His story is this: while away to negotiate for sawdust, his daughter minded the store. Possibly she was in the alley behind the store, getting rid of the animals' daily waste when the thief entered. Or perhaps she was in a back room and didn't hear the door open. At least, this is what he claims to be true."

"Do you have reason to believe otherwise?"

Holmes rocked his head back and forth to express uncertainty. "I suspect it was someone who had already been in the store that day."

I lifted slices of toast off the rack and dropped them onto his plate, then he proceeded to slather them with orange marmalade.

"Who else entered the shop?" I asked.

"Lazar said that while he was away, his daughter spoke with a customer who bought a Chinese gold-fish and the deliveryman brought fresh fruit for the animals."

"Have you questioned these people?"

"Not yet, but I will. I've arranged to meet them back at the shop later today with you, I hope."

I brightened at his remark. "Most certainly! Have you found any clues?"

"I pulled this from the chimneypiece," he said, drawing his hand out of a pocket and clutching a scrap of paper.

I took it and examined the shred. Charred black and singed brown in several places, it was decorated with a double-headed eagle and the number 10 stamped in ink on one side. "As if this was torn instead of cut, some edges not touched by fire are rough. But what does the bird signify?"

"The double-headed eagle is a historic symbol of the Hapsburgs. You may recall it from our experience which you described as 'A Scandal in Bohemia'?" With an empty plate, he crossed his silverware and sighed contentedly.

"Is this another case of foreign intrigue?"

Holmes smiled. "I would tell you my theory, but I pray you keep an open mind and follow my lead. Laszlo Lazar is from Budapest, a fact not to be forgotten. Many of his customers are immigrants, I imagine."

"If not a foreign intrigue, then simply finding a missing beast would be a trifle. Nevertheless, it's in the slightest cases where you find the most ingeniously crafted challenges."

After swallowing, his smile widened and he nodded. "Indeed!"

"Still, an albino python is expensive, isn't it?" I said.

Holmes said, "The creature is not cheap, but the greater cost is Lazar's peace of mind. When a thief can enter once, a thief may enter again. Or other thieves will follow."

"So he's paying you not just to catch a thief, but to deter others from following an example?"

"Yes," he said, "Admirable and wise, yet his anger blinds him to the simple clues of the case. This is a slight mystery, however it requires special delicacy. I'd return to Baker Street for supplies, but I need items readily in use by a medico."

I nodded. "What do you need?"

"Three vials with stoppers, some chalk dust, foolscap and gauze, and equipment for a blood stain—a needle and three slides."

I hurried to my study and gathered the items into a satchel, then kissed Mary good-bye.

It felt like old times again and stepping into the roadway, we were off in pursuit of new adventure.

The pet shop was located near the far side of Paddington Station. Its door swung outward, releasing a crowd of smells of sawdust, damp fur, and excrement. I stepped inside following Holmes's lean frame.

The walls were lined with shelves and on each shelf sat large brass cages containing olingoes, cacomistles, nigalya, civets, pangolins, and enough other exotic animals to rival Noah's ark. Frozen in mid-gesture, a stuffed and mounted monkey welcomed us inside.

"Ahoy!" Holmes called out.

The shop was one giant room with gaslight dimly accompanying bright sunshine from the plate glass windows.

"Cute little devils," I said, peering into a cage. Inside it, two kinkajou ceased their wrestling. The brown, four-footed tiny beasts looked at Holmes and me with shiny black eyes. Their foreheads were low and ears sprouted from the sides of their heads.

"You are Herr Doktor, John Vatson?" asked a man with a heavy accent. His head was bald, but a well-groomed beard and bushy eyebrows decorated his face with fiery red hair.

"Watson, may I present the proprietor, Laszlo Lazar?" Holmes said, waving his arm toward the man. "Doctor Watson is my companion on many cases, and his medical background is indispensable to the scientific inquiry of this matter."

After we shook hands, Lazar said, "I kept Ghost in the vindow."

"Ghost?" I said.

"*Da*, the albino snake. He draws a crowd at feeding time."

Along the storefront window, a wide ledge spanned the sill. On it were cages of lapdogs, various breeds of canaries, and other creatures. Interspersed between them silver stands tipped by glass globes holding Paradise Fish, swordtails, and rosy barbs. The largest cage was empty.

Pointing to the gap in the menagerie, I asked, "This is where Ghost was?"

"Papa?" A voice interrupted us. A girl no more than ten years old stepped through a back doorway wearing a scarlet frock coat with velvet sleeves and gold embroidery. Hair the colour of winter sunlight curled out from under a mobcap. Her eyes were ice blue and her skin so pale, traces of blood vessels were visible.

"Here is my daughter, Anna. I tank Gott that she was out while the thief vas here."

"Now that we've made our introductions, the vial if you please, Watson?" Holmes said.

I opened my satchel, unwrapped a glass tube, and passed it to him.

Holmes held it in one hand and gripped the stopper in his other hand. "With a sample of air, I can extract different breaths. Once I separate out the breaths through scientific means, I'll determine how many people entered the store." He held the vial high in front of him, and he wafted air over its mouth. After a dramatic flourish, he corked and handed it back to me. "Store this, but make sure the stopper doesn't come undone."

I examined the plug, re-wrapped the glass in cloth, and returned it to my satchel.

"How will you tell the breath of animals from the breath of people?" Anna asked.

Holmes raised a finger to his lips and hummed. "It will be difficult, but if I can't do it on my own, I'll ask the kind ladies of Bedford College for help. Like you, they're a clever lot—and I'm sure together we can interpret the matter."

"I see," she said.

"Of course, a confession might make things easier, especially if it were an accident or unintentional." He looked squarely at Laszlo. "Surely, it is better to forgive than to seek revenge."

While Lazar sputtered to respond, Holmes signaled with his eyes down toward Anna.

"*Da*, Anna, forgiveness is better," Lazar admitted.

"Now, we turn to the next scientific test. Watson, the chalk dust?"

We stepped over to the empty cage in the large front window. Holmes sprinkled chalk dust on the glass and gently whisked it with a new shaving brush. Spots appeared—the prints and pads of fingers. "Do you see, Watson? The ghosts of fingers."

"Due for a washing," I said.

"On the contrary, washing would remove evidence. Every fingerprint is different, and the swirls and bends of skin are like the grains of woods. Each is as unique as the signature scrawled by those very fingers."

Laszlo asked, "Once you find the thief, can you prove by his breath and his fingers that he was here?"

"There will be no room for an alibi. May I have the foolscap?" Holmes asked.

I gave him the paper.

Holmes sketched the prints. Meanwhile, the door pushed open with the jingle of bells. Into the shop walked a deep brown greatcoat housing a small man, the thick wool practically hiding his entire body. The tips of his Wellingtons poked out from under the hem and his small head stretched out above the lapels.

"Benjamin Kincaid, the last customer, I presume?" Holmes asked.

"Fellmonger and wool-stapler extraordinaire, at your service," he said.

Another man entered the shop sporting a bowler and a careworn Raglan coat. "The deliveryman, Aloysius Robinson," Lazar said. The figure tipped his hat with a wink and a grin.

As Lazar explained matters to the gentlemen, Holmes set about his preparations. He tipped an inkpot into a wad of gauze, then smeared and squeezed the fabric until it was fully saturated with ink. Next he unfurled a roll of foolscap and pressed both men's fingertips against the gauze. Then on the foolscap, fingers left a trail of black splotches.

Our silence was interrupted by random chirps and chitters punctuating the air. A macaw doused in sky blue flapped up to a high perch.

"You saw what happened," I addressed the bird. "Who abducted the white snake?"

Cocking its head, it stared through one eye. "God save the Queen," it replied.

Holmes blinked at the inkblots for several long moments then glanced between the finger-prints on the glass, Lazar, and his daughter.

An African porcupine stirred in a corner. The dark creature's white wisps of quills rustled as it walked, shaking against each other and gently scraping the side of the cage.

"Well, Holmes?" I asked.

"I'm afraid the analysis of fingerprints will require several hours of study. Even then, the results may be inconclusive. We must attempt the blood test," he said.

"Blood test?" Kincaid said. His expression puckered into a grimacing frown.

Holmes said, "This last test comes directly from medicine. As you know, when people lie, they become anxious and even agitated. Cheeks become flushed and heartbeats race. Skilled criminals calm themselves, slow their hearts and mask the clues. The body can't be silenced, however, and if a person lies, the truth can be found in a few drops of blood. If I collect a drop of blood from the thief, then I will have proof." He turned to Kincaid and asked, "Did you steal the python?"

"No, sir."

"Do you know who took it?"

Kincaid laid a hand over his heart. "On my mother's grave, Mister Holmes, I do not know."

I pricked Kincaid's finger and drew a slide.

"You may go, Mister Kincaid," Holmes said. "If you are caught in a lie, I assure you that Watson and I will crush you with the full extent of the law."

Over a serpent, however rare? I thought to myself.

When Anna looked up with widened eyes, Holmes added, "Clemency spares only those who tell the truth forthrightly. Now, to Mister Robinson."

Robinson made a sour face and held out his palm. "First you soil my fingers, now you intend to prick them?"

Holmes ignored the question. "Do you know what happened to the white snake?"

"I haven't a clue," he answered.

"Do you know who took it?"

Shaking his head, rolling his eyes, he said, "No."

I pricked his finger and smeared the blood on the glass.

"You may go," Holmes said.

"You expect me to wear my glove like this?" he said with a sneer, splaying his five blackened fingers, one growing a bead of crimson.

"There's a vashbasin in the back room," Lazar said.

When Robinson left, only Holmes and me, the shopkeeper and his daughter remained. In one cage, two coatimundi broke into a fight. The smaller one pounced on the larger one who in turn boxed its snout.

"Is it in our animal nature to cause each other problems?" I asked as we watched the tiny beasts.

"They're funny little fellows." Lazar picked up the smaller coatimundi and it looked down its snout at me through his black eye mask. "They can unscrew lids and untie knots."

"We have our own knot to untie with this theft," Holmes said. "There is just one other person left to question."

"Who's that?" Lazar asked.

Holmes's gaze fell to Anna. "The only other person in the shop."

"Me?" Anna said, startled.

Holmes said, "Granted, the needle is long and painful, but you want to help your father, don't you?"

"Yes, but…" She looked away and her lip trembled.

Holmes knelt on one knee so he was at eye-level with her. "Yes, Anna? What is it?"

She rubbed a tear out of her eye. "The snake is gone. It's my fault."

Putting a hand on her shoulder, Holmes said, "I don't understand…what do you mean?"

Her voice broke and she turned her back to us. "A man came, asking about it, so I showed it to him. He paid me, and I let him walk away with it."

"Who was this person?"

"I don't know. He said he knew you, papa, so I trusted him… but then I wondered if he deceived me."

Holmes stood up, and fished around in his pocket. "Did he pay with this?" Carefully, he lifted the shred of burnt bill. It showed the ten and double-headed eagle.

The girl nodded. "Fake money. Poppa takes in money from the old country from time to time but that is not Hungarian. It's not even Austrian or Croat."

"You thought the man tricked you, so you burned the money and tried to hide your mistake?"

The girl exclaimed, "He did trick me!"

Holmes sighed. "This is the newly minted Dalmatian ten-dinar note."

She gasped. "I'm so sorry, papa. This man gave me these paper notes and I didn't know what to do. I just took them, but I felt tricked and ashamed, so I threw them into the fire and I lied." Hiding her face, she choked back her cries.

Lazar wrapped an arm around her. "There, there now. The albino vas hardly worth a thing. It cost us dearly just to feed it and keep it alive."

Holmes smiled at the girl, then he looked at Lazar. "Don't let her marry poorly. She's intelligent enough to manage this store when she gets older—let her work and learn. This isn't a mistake, it's a lesson."

"A lesson for me, too, Mister Holmes," Lazar said. Then he laughed. "Ve are back to normal, it seems, very much tanks to you and your scientific methods."

As the setting sun poured golden light through the window, we enjoyed cigars at Baker Street. Holmes reclined in his easy chair while I nestled into the wicker basket chair. His new companion, a kinkajou from the pet shop, sat in its cage, gripping half an orange with its front paws.

"Have you ever thought about acquiring a pet, Watson?" Holmes asked.

I smiled. "I'd love a dog, but I would want an estate to hunt with it."

"Not a caged songbird or a South American parrot?" Holmes asked.

"Mary's the only company I need, and my patients require all the care and attention I can spare."

The kinkajou bit into the bowl of the half-cut orange, flashing a pink tongue. As its jaws flashed open and shut, bits of pulp dropped to the cage floor.

"It's remarkable what you did, Holmes," I said. "I didn't know that you could extract a man's breath from the air that he breathed."

He grinned. "Yes, isn't it?"

"In your other cases, I've never seen you put it to use."

With a wink, he said, "Well…it's more of a theoretical possibility than an everyday practice."

"And the whole study of finger-prints? Same 'theoretical possibility'?"

"Yes," Holmes said. "Although I didn't make that up. I attended Galton's lecture on personal identification, but have not had an opportunity to calibrate my skills to his studies."

Indeed, in a few short years, the work of William Herschel, Henry Faulds, and Francis Galton grew into a science. After his resurrection from Reichenbach Falls, he ably noted that no two thumbprints are alike in "The Adventure of the Norwood Builder."

"The blood test, though, I could almost believe, if I weren't a practicing doctor."

He nodded. "Don't mention it to the British Medical Society."

"It was all a game."

Shaking his head, he asked, "Would you rather I pointed a finger and accuse the daughter while her father boiled with anger at a thief?"

I thought while the pendulum of the clock ticked back and forth. Finally, I said, "No, but if the daughter had kept mum, your methods would have been revealed as so much quackery, and your reputation would have been ruined."

"The illusion of the science convinced her that the truth would out."

"You mentioned the women of Bedford College and warned Robinson would be 'crushed by the full extent of the law' for the girl's sake?"

He waved a hand. "Naturally."

"If the snake's purchaser knew Laszlo personally—which we can deduce, since he knew he could pay with foreign currency—then wouldn't the truth have come out over time, one way or another?"

"Yes, Watson, but we were lucky to help the daughter admit her mistake and also to make sure the father forgave her."

"How did you know it was the daughter?" I asked.

"Elementary, my dear Watson. The remains in the fireplace were the biggest clue."

I agreed. "Of course."

"Also, no cages were opened, no animals had escaped, so this concerned someone whose time wasn't devoted to fleeing, but rather someone concerned with the look of the shop."

A muffled scream erupted through the floorboards and under the hearth rug. The nearby cage was empty. "Speaking of escape, Holmes. I believe Mrs Hudson has met your new roommate."

HAPPY BIRTHDAY, MR HOLMES!

by Gary Lovisi

It was in late 1903 after the affair I would eventually chronicle as "The Adventure of the Creeping Man" for *The Strand* magazine, when my friend Sherlock Holmes seemed to be in an unusual mood of dark disturbance. I could only assume that it was the Abercrombie situation that was playing upon his mind—a dangerous escaped convict who was said to be on his way to London. Holmes would not speak of it and even the press was sparse regarding details, so I put the matter aside for the time being. I had concerns of my own just then causing me considerable consternation.

Mary, my wife, had gone away for a protracted visit to the north country to look after her ailing mother, so I found myself alone and lonely at home without her. I was much buoyed when Holmes suggested I move back into our old lodgings at Baker Street for the next month or two while she was away. It was a generous offer on his part to assuage my loneliness and I felt beholden to do something to reciprocate his generosity—and I knew exactly what I would do to repay my good friend.

"Watson? Now what is it?" Sherlock Holmes asked me with obvious disdain that morning as we finished breakfast. "I can smell the wood burning."

"Should I stoke the fire?" I asked coyly.

"Hah! Not the fireplace, old man, but you, your very thoughts. Your mind is working in high gear. I fear you may hurt yourself if you tax your faculties so harshly."

"You…fear…What?" I blurted, holding down my chagrin.

Holmes laughed, allowing a mischievous grin, "You are up to something. I can read the signs all over you, though you are trying hard to hide it. Now I wonder what it can be?"

"Really, Holmes! You can be insufferable at times."

Sherlock Holmes smiled victoriously. I knew he was playing with me now. "That does it! Now whatever can you be planning? Surely not that execrable birthday party scheme again? Each year at this time you endeavor to harass me with that ridiculous non-sense, and each year I refuse you adamantly."

"That may be, Holmes, but this is different. This January, the sixth will be your fiftieth birthday, a singular milestone in your life and career," I spoke softly, imploringly, for I knew his rages and upon this matter he had always been very firm. Nevertheless, I felt I had to press ahead for he was correct, you see, I did have plans. I added, "This is a special moment in your life. You should celebrate this occasion. I wish to celebrate it. Many people would like to celebrate it with you."

"Then do so. Tip a pint! Tip a dozen pints for all I care, but do please leave me out of it. I have no wish to be put on display, regaled by gawkers with whom I am forced to make pleasantries, while being force-fed food and victuals, then stuffed with cake or pastry, only to finally be presented with meaningless gifts—none of which I need by the way—all the time having to thank the givers profusely. I can think of nothing more loathsome. Why, I should be forced to resort to the cocaine needle or even the opium pipe to as-suage my wounded psyche. Thank you, but no thank you, Watson."

"But, Holmes…?" I stammered, then stopped abruptly for I saw his face had grown dark and grim.

My companion only shook his head sadly and suddenly flung down his *Times*, then he swiftly arose from his chair with a huff and marched into his bedroom, slamming the door firmly behind him. I believe Holmes had made his feelings quite clear to me upon the subject of birthdays, but I would not let that stop me from planning a party in his honour—whether he wanted one or not!

The next day Holmes and I were in our sitting room. He was smoking prodigiously upon his favourite pipe, creating quite the thick fog, no doubt deep in some deductive thoughts. I was quietly perusing my notes of the Carfax Case.

"Holmes?" I inquired softly.

He looked up at me and allowed a grim smile. "Absolutely not, Watson!"

"But…but…"

"No 'buts' need be applied. I know you are ignoring my wishes and are planning to have a birthday party for me here on January sixth. I know you will invite friends and even some…acquaintances…"

"Please, Holmes, be reasonable."

"Reasonable, Watson! You harm me deeply with this request. I want no party. I have never wanted a party. I never celebrate my date of birth. A ridiculous custom. Why should I begin now? In any event, do as you will, but I certainly will never attend such a gathering. Case closed."

I nodded, subdued by my friend's firm conviction, but more determined than ever to give him a party to celebrate his life, something he so richly deserved.

"Your birthday party will go on with or without you, Holmes," I stated firmly.

"Then it shall go on without me," he replied just as firmly. I could see he was immovable upon this subject, so I would have to amend my plans accordingly. My ace in the hole was his brother, Mycroft, who told me that at the right time he would call Holmes away upon some pretext.

The days passed and Holmes seemed distracted by several interesting cases that climaxed at the end of the year. The situation regarding Abercrombie I could tell was now uppermost in his mind, but he would still give me no details.

New Year's Day, 1904, saw us enjoying a lovely dinner compliments of our landlady, Mrs Hudson. She winked at me as she took away the empty dishes of our feast. She was excited by the idea of the party and naturally was the first person after Mycroft who I invited. She was overjoyed by the idea but had not let on to Holmes her excitement. I believe she was more difficult for Holmes to read than was I. Irrespective of all that, I began to grow concerned because the big event was now just five days away.

Holmes remained as obdurate as ever upon the subject.

"So, my good Watson, you thought your little plan slipped my mind in all the rush of recent cases. I assure you nothing could be farther from the truth."

"Be reasonable, Holmes," I implored once more, trying to take a different tack with him.

"Reasonable, yes, by all means, I shall be. My reasonableness extends to the promise that I shall not leave these premises the entire day of the sixth. Ah, but do not celebrate victory just yet, my friend. For I will allow no visitors to enter our rooms either. Nor will I permit you to hang one single party ribbon nor atrocious piece of celebratory bunting anywhere on these premises. If you do so, I will simply pull them down and tear them into tiny pieces. So you see, my friend, your party is effectively aborted. It shall be still-born. Now why not just admit defeat so we can put all this silliness behind us? There is a new magic act at the *Lyceum* that is all the rage, a female magician by the name of 'The Young and Lovely Lucille,' and I have obtained two tickets. What do you say?"

"So that is how you prove to be reasonable? To buy me off! I am sorry, my friend, but I do not accept your offer. January sixth marks your half century and upon my soul, a celebration of your birth will take place upon that day!"

Holmes just moaned, relit his pipe and walked over to our front window to stare down at Baker Street below. I saw him take something from his pocket, look over it carefully, then quickly put it back into his pocket. Was it the tickets or something else? I had no idea what it was about, but he looked grim now. Holmes was quiet and in deep thought and grew morose, as if struggling with something, but he would not tell me and I knew better than to ask. I knew with my friend that all things were made known in their proper time, so I did not intrude upon his thoughts. Since my marriage and moving out of Baker Street, I feared he had gone back to his old secretive ways. He was being difficult. Nevertheless, I did not care, Sherlock Holmes was going to have his birthday party if it was the last thing I ever did—but he had now put up a serious impediment to my plan.

When the morning of the sixth approached I felt that all was lost. Holmes was firmly ensconced in our rooms like some grim stone monument, unmoving, inflexible. True to his word he would allow no visitors, not even Mrs Hudson. He would not allow me to decorate the rooms. I was effectively flummoxed. I had the nightmare thought of Holmes standing steadfastly behind our locked door all that evening, chiding our guests by not allowing them to enter. Some of the people I invited were coming from quite a distance. It was looking as if all my plans would end up in utter disaster.

Mycroft was essential to my plans, but upon the morning of the party his scheme to get Sherlock out of our rooms upon some pretext proved futile. Holmes would not bite. He would not take the bait Mycroft dangled before him and leave our rooms. What was I to do? And guests would be arriving later that very evening, just hours away.

As the day wore on my nerves grew more frayed. Holmes just sat there calmly smoking up a storm, a whimsical smile playing across his face as he watched me in my agitated state of quiet dismay. I quite believe he was enjoying my distress. The scoundrel!

The morning passed badly. Later Mrs Hudson brought us up a light luncheon. Holmes graciously allowed her to enter our rooms and she quietly placed the meal tray down before us. She shot me an inquiring look and when Holmes was distracted her lips made the silent words, "What is happening?" I shook my head negatively. Nothing was happening. I could well understand her concern, but I was nonplussed by Holmes's activity—or lack of it. He would not leave our rooms and I realized by doing so, he had effectively stymied all my party plans.

I had to get Holmes out of our rooms so I could decorate them, then bring up the food and punch that Mrs Hudson had secreted below, and I had to do this all before our guests arrived. Then, even more difficult—I had to somehow get Holmes to come back to 221B. That was the real rub—but I would worry about that later, as I was looking to Mycroft to help me with that obstacle.

After a quiet lunch, the early afternoon was too soon upon us and I was simply jittery with nerves, though trying hard not to let it show. I did not want to give Holmes the satisfaction. For his part, my friend continued smoking and watched me with a rather whimsical leer upon his face. He was quite enjoying my discomfiture and openly taunted me with quick jibes, inquiring how the party was shaping up and if all was in readiness, reminding me that time was growing short.

"You can be abominable sometimes," I stated, anger covering my hurt pride.

Holmes just sat there glowing in my distress. He even had the effrontery to ask, "Do you need any help decorating?"

"No, thank you!" I barked, quite upset now that he was obviously doing all he could to make me squirm. He was baiting me.

Well, I would have none of it, but I forced myself to calm down. I took a deep breath, sighed and asked, "Holmes?"

"No, Watson, not at all," he stated firmly, but then I was surprised to see him get up from his chair, walk over to the door and put on his coat. Now what, I thought?

"I think I need to get a bit of fresh air," Holmes suddenly informed me in a firm tone. "The air in here is a bit stuffy, I believe I will go out for a walk. I shan't return before the early morning of the seventh, Watson, so have your party if you must, but know that I shall not be in attendance."

Then Sherlock Holmes left our rooms. I ran over to the front window and saw him walking briskly down Baker Street. I sighed, gathered myself together, astounded by this sudden action but overjoyed, for this was just the break I had hoped for. I immediately called down to our landlady that we were to begin to set the party in motion.

"Mrs Hudson, he's gone out, the party is on! Full speed ahead!"

"Jolly good, Doctor Watson! Jolly good!"

Mrs Hudson proved a bounty of excellent ideas. First, she helped me move the chairs and sofa out of our sitting room and into Holmes's bedroom to create more open space. My bedroom would be used for the hats and coats of our guests. Then we moved our breakfast table in front of the fireplace, which created a large open area for guests to mingle. Soon afterwards our landlady brought up plate after plate of enticing finger sandwiches along with her famous rum punch. The guests began to arrive promptly at the prearranged hour of seven o-clock.

Inspectors Lestrade of Scotland Yard was the first on the scene, accompanied by Inspector Tobias Gregson. They were old friends who had known Holmes for almost twenty years, since the case I had chronicled as *A Study in Scarlet* back in '87. Also from Scotland Yard were Inspectors Alec MacDonald, the younger Stanley Hopkins and MacKinnon, whom Holmes felt showed great promise and referred to as "Mr Mac." While it was good to see them all, I thought it a bit odd since my invitation had only gone out to Lestrade. Now there seemed to be many more men of the law arriving than I invited and I barely knew what to do about it. I finally shrugged and accepted it in good order, putting it down to Holmes's long years of work with the police.

Then Wiggins and his small gang of former street ruffians appeared, whom Holmes liked to call his Baker Street Irregulars. Various others entered the house and our rooms; former clients, people who Holmes had come into contact with over the years. There were so many. It was good to see Holmes's old friend from Oxford, Reginald Musgrave once again, whose strange problem I had written up as "The Musgrave Ritual" so many years ago; as well as my old friend 'Young' Stamford, older now and a distinguished medical man. Stamford was the fellow who had first introduced me to Holmes so many years before. Mycroft Holmes appeared soon afterwards. I was happy to see him, and to see that tonight's party was important enough for him to uproot himself from his sedentary seat in the Diogenes Club.

"Is Sherlock here yet?" the elder Holmes brother asked me, Sherlock's senior by seven years. He immediately turned towards the refreshments table and liberally partook of Mrs Hudson's exquisite rum punch—which was proving to be the hit of the evening. Soon the room filled with still more guests, all of whom were talking softly in little clusters, all seemingly sharing their favourite Sherlock Holmes story or memory. I felt sad that the great man himself would not be here for any of this celebration and that he would miss it all. It was a shame.

"I'm afraid your brother will not be coming," I told Mycroft Holmes glumly.

I looked around the rooms. They were nicely decorated—Mrs Hudson and I had done a credible job. The party was going full force, with even our bedrooms and the outer landing and stairway filling up with happy chatting guests.

"Oh, I think not, Doctor Watson," Mycroft told me with a little smile. "I am sure brother Sherlock could never resist such an event, all his protestations aside. However, you may be correct, he certainly is not the birthday type."

"I know that only too well." I blurted, my eyes scanning the rooms and outer landing. Something was not right. There seemed to be many more guests than I had ever invited. Though I scanned every face visible to me, I did not see my friend at all. I looked inquiringly at the elder Holmes.

"I do not see Sherlock anywhere."

Mycroft smiled indulgently. "Perhaps he is in disguise?"

"Disguise? Of course!" I blurted. Yes, of course, that had to be it! The wily scoundrel was in disguise. Holmes's ego would not allow him to resist being present at his own party so he could investigate all the goings on—but it never occurred to me that he would do so in disguise. I simply assumed he would arrive later, as would any other person, when the party was going full throttle and make some grand entrance. I hadn't thought that he might already be here, right this very minute. I looked over all the faces once again. I quickly discounted the Scotland Yard inspectors and others I knew by sight, but there seemed to be an alarming number of guests I did not know at all. Men and even women I had never seen before. That was perplexing. Who were all these people? Where had they all come from? There were also a number of rather flirtatious woman present. What were they doing here? I was confused. I planned for a rather small gathering, an intimate party, not this! It was rapidly turning into a three-ring circus. Holmes's great popularity had apparently grown beyond even my own comprehension.

"Can you tell me which of these men is your brother?" I asked Mycroft hopefully.

"No, Doctor, I do not see him here," Mycroft replied with a wry grin.

"Then how do I find him?" I asked hopelessly.

"If he is here at all, you must use the deductive methods you have learned from brother Sherlock. If you do so I am certain you cannot go wrong, Dr Watson." Then Mycroft Holmes walked off with a glass of rum punch to speak to someone who appeared to be a member of the royal family, who was speaking to a man I knew to be the French ambassador.

Now I was in a quandary. Holmes had apparently secretly stole into his own birthday party but was here in disguise and I could not find him. I was sure the fiend was doing this just to annoy me. I feared he might not ever reveal himself, which would certainly put a dampener upon the party. It was all up to me now.

Once again I looked over each of the guests. Some certainly appeared to be rather disreputable examples of the lower classes— or even of the criminal classes. I wondered how many might be burglars, forgers, pick-pockets, or confidence men. I was aghast. I even recognized one man who Holmes had been instrumental in having arrested, wily Jack Thomas, the pocket picker. He, at least, was harmless. I sighed, what was going on here? Then I saw another man who seemed familiar to me. I assumed he was one of the reformed criminals who sometimes aided Holmes. Maybe he knew something? I sidled up to him.

"Glad you could make Mr Holmes's party," I stated. Then I introduced myself.

"I knows who you be, I seen you with Mr 'Olmes 'pon occasion. I helps him sometimes. Me name be Rafferty."

"Rafferty? Just Rafferty?"

"Rafferty will do for today, eh?" he responded with a snicker, showing a mouth full of blackened teeth. Wherever Holmes had met such a disreputable rogue I feared to imagine.

"Well, Mr Rafferty…"

"No mister, just Rafferty," he corrected me, quite adamant upon the matter. He showed me a fierce demeanour and I grew nervous.

I took a step back, wondering if I might not need my revolver before this evening was over. Had this man come here to…burgle the house? No, my alarm was unnecessary. He was a reformed criminal, who told me he now worked with my companion, so he should prove safe. At least I hoped so. However, as I looked around the room at all the unknown faces, it dawned upon me that there were many people who might wish to do harm to my friend and one of them might even be here at this very party. The thought chilled me.

I decided to put this Rafferty fellow to the test.

"So you have done some work for Mr Holmes?" I asked, looking at him closely.

"That I does, 'pon occasion, as it warrants."

"Then perhaps you can help me?"

"If I am able, depending 'pon what it be."

I nodded, then I drew the man in close to me and whispered in his ear. "Listen, Sherlock Holmes is here, but he is in disguise. Can you point him out to me?"

"That is not for me to say. If Mr 'Olmes desires not to be known, he should remain so. He may be working on one of those cases of his," Rafferty explained in a conspiratational whisper.

I'm afraid I grew exasperated by his defiance. "Oh, come now, my man, this is a birthday party, Holmes is not working on any case. He is just trying to get my goat, punish me for giving him a party that he never wanted."

The man shrugged and then left me to converse with a group of young ladies. Now who these ladies were I had no idea. I noticed all were rather comely, and if truth be told, well-endowed and quite fetching. I shook my head in despair and forgot the ladies. I was a married man now, my Mary was away, and my friend Sherlock Holmes was doing his best to make me out a fool. Soon each of the guests was coming over to me and asking when Sherlock Holmes would appear. When, indeed!

I was in a quandary.

"Any luck yet?" Mycroft asked as he passed me with someone who looked like the prime minister.

"No, but who are all these people? I invited no more than two dozen guests but I have discovered people all throughout our rooms, out on the landing, the stairway, down through Mrs Hudson's entire first floor, and even outside in front of 221. What is going on here?"

"My brother is quite the popular fellow," Mycroft answered with a jolly laugh, then he left to refill his glass with more rum punch.

I watched him walk off and shook my head in despair. I was in a real dilemma.

Gregson and Lestrade next walked over to me. "When will Mr Holmes arrive?"

"Soon," I answered, then begged off, telling them that I had to speak with another guest on the other side of the room.

It was then that my eyes locked onto an elderly clergyman. He was tall and lean, with long grey hair under a large black slough hat. He carried a book with him under his arm. Probably a *Bible*. He was talking briskly with one of the ladies. Now here was someone of interest. Hello! Holmes had once used this very disguise years ago in the Adler Affair. I looked more closely at the old cleric. Yes, it made sense. This could certainly be Holmes. My heart leapt with joy, I had him now! I would show him!

I watched the clergyman more carefully. Yes, it could be Holmes, in fact, it had to be Holmes! I looked around for Mycroft, but he was nowhere in sight, so I decided to beard Sherlock myself. I approached the elderly clergyman and stood boldly in front of him. I stared him down. He looked back at me as if he had never seen me before. Just as I assumed he would.

I said boldly, "Holmes, I must compliment you upon your fine disguise, the old weathered face, the lank messy hair, the crazed look in the eyes, but I saw right through it immediately. I have found you out, you scoundrel!"

The old cleric looked at me uncomprehendingly, and it annoyed me that my friend would not admit defeat and insisted upon keeping up his sham in spite of my discovering his charade.

With some annoyance the cleric said, "Disguise? What disguise, young man? I am sorry, sir, but I quite do not know what you mean."

"You old rascal! Come now, admit I found you out!" I said rather loudly, insisting he come clean with the truth, sure that I had breached his disguise. We were attracting a crowd.

"Come now, sir. Doctor Watson, is it not? This is most unusual."

"You know who *I* am, and I know who *you* are, you wily rogue, you!"

"Well, this is very unseemly behaviour. I have been invited here for a party to celebrate Mr Holmes's auspicious day and now I find myself verbally accosted by some loud-mouthed mountebank! This is nothing short of outrageous!"

"*Mountebank!* Why, you old faker, I'll show you!" I blurted in anger. A crowd had definitely gathered around us now. The men from Scotland Yard, that Rafferty fellow, a tall overweight man who appeared to be a common labourer, another man in a military uniform, Wiggins and Mrs Hudson, all were looking to see what I would do next.

"Answer me, Holmes! I've had quite enough of your obtuse behavior, making a fool out of me by coming in secret to your own party and calling *me* a mountebank!"

"Mountebank is the least of it! You are an impertinent scoundrel, sir!" the old cleric barked in anger.

"Oh, be quiet, Holmes!" I shouted. "I am furious with you. Why, it would serve you right if I just pulled that fake beard right off your face!"

The elderly cleric took a step back, I took a step forward, but then I felt a firm hand upon my shoulder. I turned to find Mycroft Holmes standing beside me. He bowed down and gently whispered into my ear, "I'm afraid you have the wrong man, Doctor. That is the Reverend Mathias James of St Catherine's. I invited him here myself. My brother did some little favour for him regarding the pilfering of the church's poor box last month. He only wished to express his gratitude."

I was utterly embarrassed. I could barely stand there in front of all those people. Thankfully, by then the crowd had moved off and the general party conversation resumed. I well imagined I was the subject of much of that conversation. I took a deep breath and looked to the elder Holmes.

"Not Sherlock?" I asked in a deflated tone.

"Indeed not," Mycroft replied firmly. Then he pulled me away with him. "Come Doctor, you need some of this rum punch, your nerves seem frayed. Too much excitement for one evening, I gather. The party is simply smashing by the way, a very interesting group and they all seem to be having a fine time of things. You are to be congratulated."

I walked off numbly following Mycroft, my mind in a whirl. That poor old reverend. I would have to apologize to him later. My God, I had come one heartbeat away from pulling his whiskers right off his face!

"By the way, Doctor, do you have any idea when my brother will show himself?" the elder Holmes asked me confidentially.

I looked at him curiously. "What do you mean? I thought you said he was here, but in disguise?"

"I said he *might* be here, *perhaps* in disguise," Mycroft told me.

"So he is not here?" I asked.

"Apparently he is not," Mycroft replied simply.

I felt deflated, defeated, and suddenly very sad.

Mycroft handed me a glass of rum punch. I grasped it eagerly and in four long swallows emptied the glass. The warmth of the rum and the sweetness of the fruit did much to restore my spirits.

"What now?" I asked.

"Be patient," Mycroft said, and then he walked off to speak with the tall uniformed military man I had seen earlier.

I quickly took another glass of rum punch, my nerves were frazzled and I needed the drink. I'd not only made a fool of myself in front of everyone, I'd practically scared the daylights out of poor old Reverend James. He must think me quite insane. This party was certainly not turning out as I had planned.

As the night wore on the talk became louder, the laughter more raucous and no one left 221B. Everyone it seemed was waiting for Sherlock Holmes to make his grand entrance to celebrate his fiftieth birthday. No one was more anxious for that event to occur than I.

I decided to make the rounds, and after a few more doses of Mrs Hudson's delightful elixir—she seemed to keep the punch bowl and trays of food endlessly supplied—I loosened up somewhat and spoke to some of the guests. I focused especially on those guests I did not know. There were quite a few of them; men of apparently all backgrounds and stations in life. I introduced myself to one and all, looking to see if any of them might be Holmes in disguise. I was much more careful this time. Yet while it seemed that none of them could be Holmes, each one asked me when the guest of honour was slated to appear. I smiled and mumbled something about him having been called away earlier in the day on some important business, but that he would surely be here soon.

"Rest assured," I told one and all, with a rum punch grin, "Sherlock Holmes would never miss his own birthday party."

They all laughed and said that was certainly true.

I laughed with them as I walked away. I was a desperate man now. What to do? Where was Holmes? Why was he doing this to me?

Someone was tugging at my sleeve. "Excuse me, Doctor Watson, but can you tell me when Mr Holmes is going to show up? You know the hour is getting rather late."

The same question was put to me by an ever growing amount of guests until it became a veritable chant. "Where is Holmes! Where is Holmes!"

I swallowed hard, took a deep breath. It looked like I would have to do something soon. But what? It was obvious to me now that Holmes was not going to show up —and if by some miracle he was even here—he was not going to show himself. It looked like it fell to me to do the best I could as matters now stood.

I took another deep breath and marshaled my thoughts. Speaking in my best booming voice, I announced to one and all, "My friends, ladies and gentlemen, friends of Sherlock Holmes, the hour is getting late. I am afraid to tell you that Sherlock Holmes is away on a case and will not be able to join us, so we should have our cake now and then call it a night."

There were the expected murmurs of shock and disappointment.

"I am truly sorry that Mr Holmes is not able to be with us tonight, but he sends his regrets, regards, and he thanks you all for doing him such an honour on his birthday. I am sorry that I have let you down."

There were more murmurs of disappointment, some signs of regret. My announcement about Holmes spread a pall over the formerly joyous party. Now a hush had overcome the guests, joined by a low murmur as they all looked towards me, some not too kindly. I realized something more was called for.

I boldly moved to the front of the room, looked at the guests and spoke the only way I knew how, from my heart. "My friends, my good friends, honoured guests, we have joined here tonight to celebrate the fiftieth year of the birth of our good friend Sherlock Holmes. It is fitting we do this. It matters not that Holmes is unable to join us. Holmes is a man who has touched all our lives and in that way he is with us always. He is a man who has made the world a better place, and without him and his work as a consulting detective, we would all be worse off. I known I would be. On a personal note, Sherlock Holmes is my dear friend. He is the most decent man I have ever met. My life without him would be lost. I miss him being here tonight as much as you all do. I am sure the only reason he is not here with us tonight is because he is engaged in important work that may be a matter of life and death. You can rest assured that once I see him I shall chide him without mercy for his absence!" There was a bit of light laughter by the guests at that remark and I smiled. I was winning the crowd. Then I continued, "What I do know, is that were Sherlock Holmes here, he would be overcome by this outpouring of love and affection that you all show him. So many old friends are here together again, and all to honour him. Holmes would be deeply touched and thank you all."

There was a cheer and then clapping and I quickly wiped the sweat that streamed down my face.

"I think it is time. Now let's have our cake!" I announced to raucous cheers. "Mrs Hudson!"

By then, of course, everyone was swarming around me, each one wishing Holmes good cheer and congratulations. Lestrade, Gregson and all the Scotland Yard inspectors, Wiggins and his gang, Stamford, Reginald Musgrave, various clients, and even some men Holmes had put away. All offered their good wishes. I noticed another Stamford offer his congratulations, Archie Stamford the forger, and then Mycroft stepped up and shook my hand.

"Well done, Doctor Watson, well done indeed!" the elder Holmes told me and I beamed with pride.

Then the crowd suddenly parted as a familiar female voice called out boldly in a loud Scottish accent, "Come on now, move off, make room! Coming through!"

It was Mrs Hudson holding a large chocolate cake set ablaze with candles – fifty of them if I am not mistaken. She deftly placed the cake down upon the table in front of us.

"Seeing as Mr Holmes is not present, Doctor Watson, why don't you make a wish for him and then blow out the candles," she stated. Then she ordered, "Hurry up or the cake will melt and everyone is waiting for a piece."

I took a minute to look around at all the faces beaming with good cheer and I do believe my eyes misted up for just a moment. At that instance I missed Holmes greatly, so sorry he was missing this celebration in his honour. Then I quickly took a deep breath and blew out all the candles in one great gust of wind.

Instantly those in the room, and all those throughout the entire house, let out with a raucous chant:

"HAPPY BIRTHDAY, MR HOLMES!!!"

I was obviously touched by the emotion exhibited for my friend and simply said, "Thank you all, Sherlock Holmes thanks you all!"

Then Mrs Hudson cut the cake and began handing it out to the guests on her prized china.

Wiggins then came over to me on the sly. He was the one who put me on the right track.

"Eh, Doctor Watson, you 'ear from Mr 'Olmes yet?"

"You know I have not, you rascal," I replied a bit short with the young man. I'd known Wiggins since he had been a young pup, just a boy—one of those Holmes liked to call his 'Irregulars.'

"Well 'e told me you should be on the lookout for Abercrombie," Wiggins said in a low tone.

"You spoke with Holmes? Where is he?" I asked quietly. "Point him out to me now!"

"I cannot, 'e told me this yesterday and I've not seen nor 'eard from 'im since."

"Abercrombie?" I said softly. That meant something. The escaped convict. Here! What was that about? I looked at Wiggins. "Did he tell you what this Abercrombie looked like or why I should be on the watch for him."

"No, sir, just that you should keep your eyes open and stay away from him."

I shook my head in frustration. How could I look out for this Abercrombie or stay away from him when I did not even know what the man looked like? And a dangerous escaped convict at that! Then my eyes spotted the Scotland Yard inspectors talking heatedly in a small circle apparently about old cases and having a fine time of it—Lestrade, Gregson, Hopkins, MacDonald, and the man Holmes liked to call 'Mr Mac.'

I smiled as I entered their midst, "Gentlemen!"

"Fine party, Doctor Watson," Lestrade said as he downed more punch and picked up another sandwich.

"Simply smashing!" Hopkins added with a grin. It appeared the rum punch already had some effect on him—as it was having on most of the guests.

"Gentlemen, perhaps you can help me?" I asked cordially. "Have any of you heard of the escaped convict, Abercrombie?"

"Dangerous man," Mr Mac stated seriously.

"Murderer with no pity," Gregson added.

I gulped nervously. Those were not the words I wanted to hear, but I expected no less.

"Do any of you know what the man looks like? Could you pick him out in a crowd?" I asked hopefully.

All five inspectors looked dubious and shook their heads in the negative.

Hopkins then explained, "Abercrombie has always appeared the same, shaved round head, clean shaved face, even his eyebrows are shaved. He's been on the run for over a month, ample time to change his appearance, so unless you see a man matching that description, you'll never find him. He is probably on a ship to America or Australia at this very moment."

"I hope so," I said.

Then they asked about my interest in him. I shrugged and just replied that I had read of him in the press and it was a passing fancy.

I next tried Mycroft and he was also of no help. I found myself back where I had started.

I looked over at the many men in the room, then thought of all the other men throughout the house. I knew that there could easily be a dozen or more men who might be Abercrombie. Which one was he? Abercrombie, the escaped convict! Why was he here? I nodded, now convinced, there could be but one reason. Abercrombie was here to kill Sherlock Holmes!

A deadly chill ran through me. There really was much more to this party than met the eye and if Holmes was truly here, I now hoped he *was* in disguise and would not reveal himself.

I walked through the rooms and the outer landing, down the stairs and even to the outside steps of 221 for any sign of Holmes— or a man who might be my friend in disguise. There was no one. Where was he? And this Abercrombie! What of him? Obviously, the two were stalking each other in some mad dance of criminal pursuit and criminal revenge. I began to fear for my friend and told my feelings to Mycroft.

"I feel terrible," I told the elder Holmes. "I never thought that Sherlock taking on a disguise might be for some other reason— that it was a matter of life and death."

"Fear not, good doctor. Sherlock has all well in hand."

"Where is he then?" I asked nervously.

"I think it may be time. Did you notice the military officer in the red uniform?" Mycroft asked me, a slight smile playing across his lips.

"Sherlock?" I whispered softly.

Mycroft did not answer that question, instead he told me, "He is Colonel Sir Ralph Richards. As I say, an interesting fellow. Perhaps you would like me to introduce you to him?"

I nodded. Being a retired Army doctor, I was always eager to meet another military man. Mycroft took me to where the Colonel was apparently holding court. He was busy speaking with various guests, including Reverend James, that Rafferty fellow, and a disreputable man who appeared to be nothing more than some heavy oaf, a down-and-out ne'er-do-well who had apparently crashed the party for the free food and beverages supplied so amply by Mrs Hudson. He wolfed down food and drink as if he had never seen such victuals before. Well, so be it. The poor fellow was apparently hungry. I quickly turned away from the man to look at the other guests.

In a voice loud enough for all to hear, Mycroft Holmes said, "Colonel Sir Ralph Richards, I would like to present to you a good friend of my brother's, and our host for the evening, Doctor John H Watson."

The Colonel and I shook hands and exchanged pleasantries. I looked carefully at this military man and was perplexed. He could be Holmes in disguise. He was tall and lean, but the uniform covered much. The cap and longish black hair, the large moustache and mutton-shop whiskers all seemed to disguise him quite well. *If* it was Holmes. I was not quite sure, especially after my run-in with the Reverend James, who was nearby and watching me closely as if I were some escapee from Bedlam about to go on the bonkers without a moment's notice. I saw the Reverend take a careful step back. I sighed.

I was considering the possibility that the Colonel might just be Holmes in disguise when that party-crashing oaf, apparently fully drunk and now disorderly to boot, lost his balance and bumped me hard, pushing me with a wild fall into that Rafferty fellow. Well, that fellow got angry and pushed me back even harder. I lost my balance. There was a tussle, a confusion of arms and legs. I tried to apologize for my clumsiness, but just then other men got involved and curses and fists began to fly. I cannot explain how it all happened, but the Colonel, the large labourer, Rafferty, the Reverend, myself, and even Mycroft ended up in some confused mêlée of kicking feet and flying fists. When it was all over, the Colonel lay upon the floor apparently stunned. I immediately ran over to offer him medical attention—one military man to another. Mycroft quickly called over the men from Scotland Yard. I was shocked. Certainly as gentlemen we could work out this little mix-up among ourselves without bringing in the police?

I helped the Colonel to his feet, but just then the large labourer and that Rafferty lout firmly pushed me aside, away from the poor man.

"What is the meaning of this!" I barked.

"We'll take it from here, Watson." The voice of Sherlock Holmes spoke suddenly, though I did not see him anywhere. I looked quickly into the faces of the men around me but did not see him.

Mycroft just smiled.

The Reverend James glared at me.

Then I saw the Colonel briskly being handed over to Gregson and Lestrade by of all people that Rafferty fellow, who was holding up a wicked-looking knife that he had apparently found concealed in the Colonel's uniform. Rafferty held up the knife and gave it to Lestrade, saying, "'ere you go, the knife he planned to plant into Mr 'Olmes's 'eart!'

I looked at him, aghast. What was the meaning of this? Rafferty was aided in this action by that large oaf, the party-crashing labourer. I barely knew what to make of it all. Then I heard the voice again.

"Over here, Watson."

"Where?" I said and turned to look upon Rafferty. He smiled at me, showing blackened teeth, then he pointed to the large oaf beside him. The labourer. I did a double take.

"Hello, Watson," the man said simply.

"Hello. Holmes? Is it truly you?" I asked in awe, watching as a miraculous transformation quickly took place before my eyes. The man I thought to be some heavy drunken labourer who crashed Holmes's party for the food and rum, began to shed his disguise. I watched with astonishment as he suddenly withdrew multiple wads of padding from his waist to slim down appreciably. He became rail thin.

"Yes, good old Watson, it is I," the man said. I watched with astonishment as he took off a fake nose, removed his faux whiskers, and withdrew something from his mouth that had distorted his entire face. The man before me was, in fact, my friend Sherlock Holmes.

"How? Why?" I stammered, full of questions. "And the Colonel?"

"Not the Colonel, but Miles Abercrombie come here to murder me," Holmes explained. "I put the man away years ago and upon his escape he came here to pay me back in kind."

I looked at my friend in awe, "I can't believe it is you, Holmes!"

"Believe, Watson," he said with a wry smile.

"And—that Rafferty fellow? Who the blazes is he? For a while I even thought he might be you in disguise," I stated, now watching Lestrade and Gregson busy putting manacles upon the Colonel— I mean Abercrombie. Then two stout bobbies came to escort the man out of 221B and back to prison.

"Ah, yes, Mr Rafferty…" Holmes mused thoughtfully.

"Just Rafferty, if you please, Mr 'Olmes," he blurted with a lopsided grin.

"Yes, Rafferty. Well, Watson, perhaps you remember Shinwell "Porky" Johnson from the Illustrious Client Case of two years previous? I did a bit of disguise work on his face as well but I am sure he must have looked familiar to you."

"Indeed he did, Holmes, but I could not place him. So Mr Johnson was your partner in this case?" I asked, somewhat hurt by the realization.

Sherlock Holmes laughed gently, put his hand firmly upon my shoulder and said, "Good old Watson, no one can ever replace you, but I could not allow you to be placed in such jeopardy with Abercrombie running lose. In any event it was hardly a case at all. Porky is a hardened street tough and a good stout fellow in a brawl. I was sure I might have need of his skills to take down Abercrombie—before he took me down."

"You were playing a dangerous game, Holmes."

"Indeed, Watson, Miles Abercrombie is a deadly fellow, but your party scheme proved to be the ideal cover for what I had in mind. It all worked out quite well, allowing me to smoke him out of hiding where he could be recaptured," Holmes stated. Then he added, "But I apologize for being so difficult with you about the party. Please be assured it was all done for your own protection. The less you knew about this little problem, the better for your safety—always a matter paramount in my mind, old friend."

Holmes's words touched my heart and they did much to assuage my anger over his actions the recent month. Now that he had taken off all of his disguise, he was the fellow I always recognized.

"Sorry, Watson, but when Mycroft sent me this intelligence I went to Lestrade to invite these men here. I do not like parties at all, but this one certainly went as I would have wished. By the way,

I did rather enjoy your little speech, though it rang a bit too much like a eulogy for my taste. I thank you for your kind words, but I am not quite ready for retirement yet—permanent or otherwise."

"Of course." I smiled, then looked at my friend and asked, "Well, now that it is done, will you at least have a glass of rum punch with me to celebrate your fiftieth birth year?"

Holmes's smile was broad and warm, "Why, I would be delighted, Watson. You know, you really have done a fine job on this party."

"Well, Mrs Hudson helped," I said as we clinked our glasses together. Then I said, "Happy birthday, Sherlock."

"Thank you, John," he said, and we downed our drinks.

There was then a brief moment of silence between the two of us, just two old friends, sharing a drink together.

Holmes smiled broadly. "I really must commend Mrs Hudson on her rum punch, it has quite the kick."

"I had her make it especially for you."

"Well, Watson, you and Mrs Hudson excelled with this party—in all of its aspects. I thank you sincerely."

"It is nothing, my friend," I replied, grasping his shoulder in good fellowship.

"No, it is very much something, and I truly thank you for it." Holmes spoke softly to me, then in a much firmer voice he added, "Especially since this is the last time I will ever allow you to throw me a birthday party."

"We shall see about that!" I replied with a laugh.

"Yes, we shall," Holmes gently chided, "but for now let us eat a piece of that delicious-looking cake. I swear you have put Mrs Hudson's homemaking abilities to the test this evening, but she has come through with flying colours, as usual."

"Why thank you, Mr Holmes..." Mrs Hudson broke in with evident delight. For once it appeared she was getting the last word as she quickly passed my friend a plate with a large piece of chocolate cake upon it. Then she gently kissed his cheek and said, "... and a very happy birthday to you, Mr Holmes."

✗

THE ADVENTURE OF THE ECCENTRIC INVENTOR

by Eugene D. Goodwin

It was early in 1891 when my friend Sherlock Holmes and I met one of the most unusual persons we'd ever encountered. That he was a genius is undeniable, though he was indeed an eccentric one. By now, all the world has heard of him; he invented many significant things that have had enormous impact upon modern society. His name: Nikola Tesla. When he entered our parlour at 221B Baker Street, he was just thirty-five years old, though we did not find that out till much later.

Mrs Hudson announced him. A tall man entered. He had the piercing, reflective eyes of one used to self-communing. He had a neatly-trimmed mustache and a smile replete with irony. His clothing was dapper and, I surmised, rather costly. "Dear Mr Holmes and Dr Watson," said he, "I am Nikola Tesla."

We leapt to our feet, exclaiming encomiums to his undeniable genius.

With a smile, he thanked us. "I have not come here to dwell upon my achievements, though I think I may be excused for showing some little pride in various of my accomplishments. But the reason that I have wished to meet you both—yes, Dr Watson, I did say *both!* Your splendid histories of Mr Holmes's adventures in *The Strand* are why I have elected to come here today. You see, gentlemen—now isn't that an interesting word? It's meaning is, of course, obvious, yet Shakespeare also equated it with 'Gentile.'"

"Indeed, yes," Holmes replied. "That would be in the fourth act of *The Merchant of Venice*. I've played the Venetian Duke, and it is he who speaks that line."

Tesla nodded. "Correct. But I digress. The reason I am here—"

"Is because you believe something has been stolen from you."

A bit of a gasp. "You are indeed this good doctor's protagonist! Then you know—"

"Not all that much," Holmes continued. "Merely that you do not live in London, but in New York—not the state—oh, sorry! Of course you do. What I meant—"

"Is that I make my home in Manhattan."

"Thank you. Yes, at the New Yorker Hotel at—I believe—34th Street at Eighth Avenue."

Tesla turned to me and said, "As delightful as your accounts are, they hardly do Mr Holmes justice."

I laughed ruefully. "He has pointed that out to me on more than one occasion."

"Well, sir," Tesla said to Holmes, "I venture to suppose that you might be able to tell some other things about me?"

"Let's see." Holmes ticked off points on his fingertips. "One, you were born in Serbia. Two, you have invented—or, rather, discovered—alternating current. Three, you adore pigeons. Four, you live a spartan existence. And fifth and last, you seem to have acquired a formidable enemy."

Our guest blanched. "Right on all counts. Of course, it is common knowledge where I was born and where I now reside. It is equally well known that I have brought about what is commonly referred to as—"

"A C," I said.

"Yes, my good doctor. But to proceed, while my love for pigeons has often been noted and reported, my spartan existence, as Mr Holmes calls it, is not all that well known, for I am a rather private person. Yet I suppose some hint of my habits has appeared in print." He took a deep breath. "But as for my enemy—"

Holmes held up a hand to forestall him. "Before we get into that, Mr Tesla, may I offer you a glass of wine or something stronger?"

"Thank you, but I do not drink. I used to once, but now I regard alcohol as unhealthy."

"In that case," Holmes said, "I doubt that you smoke, either."

"Great Heavens, no!" He shuddered. "I would sooner take a shot of scotch. It is a habit surely injurious to one's lungs and I think it can and has proven fatal."

Holmes sighed. "Would it discomfit you if I lit my pipe?"

"No, not at all," he replied, though I suspect he was not pleased at the prospect. As Holmes lit up and began to puff, he suggested we return to the question of Tesla's enemy.

"It is a man whom I have known for perhaps five or six years. We began as friends, which he still pretends to be, and he—"

"—is Thomas—"

"Please, Mr Holmes, do not speak his name. But since you know who we are dealing with, how should we proceed?"

Holmes said, "Before I answer that, it would be helpful if we knew the nature of what has gone missing."

"If I tell you this, may I be assured of your discretion?"

"Watson and I will never say a word about it, not even to Mrs Hudson."

"Very well. It is a formidable secret weapon; it is not theoretical, it already exists."

With a slight shake of his head and a deep sigh, Holmes said, "I am afraid that I must now inform you that your enemy is not the person you think he is. It is someone much, much worse. By comparison, your former friend is a bit of puff pastry." He turned to me. "Yes, Watson, you are correct in your assumption."

"Then both of you are aware of him," Tesla observed. "What is his name?"

"For your own protection, I must not reveal that. The most that I may tell you is that he is a mathematics professor with the initials J M."

"That tells me almost nothing."

Holmes dashed out the contents of his pipe and somewhat acerbically replied, "You must trust me, sir."

"Yes, but—"

My friend shook his head, but then added, "Mr Tesla, did you ever hear of a master criminal of many years back whose name was Jonathan Wild?"

A nod. "He was the inspiration for Mr Peachum in John Gay's *The Beggar's Opera*, as well as the title character of Henry Fielding's novel, *Jonathan Wild*."[1]

"Correct. London thought Wild was on the side of the law. The man who arranged to steal your plans patterns himself on Jonathan Wild. He has organized nearly all crime in England, as well as

---

1   Wild was also the model for Peachum in Bertolt Brecht's *The Three-Penny Opera*, as well as the villainous Arnold Zeck in a trio of murder mystery novels featuring the Mycroft-sized New York City consulting detective Nero Wolfe; its author was Rex Stout.

Scotland and Wales, though not Ireland." [Holmes didn't explain how he knew this, but it is because Moriarty has an Irish brother who is a Catholic priest. Details are in "The Revenge of the Fenian Brotherhood," transcribed by Miss Carole Buggé, elsewhere in this issue. –Ed.]

Holmes continued. "This professor covers his traces so well that even my brother Mycroft, who knows all that goes on in England, never heard of him till I gave him warning."

Tesla shuddered. "How may we combat such a formidable foe?"

"We don't. Anything that we do must be on as hushed a level as we can manage, and as inconspicuously as possible. Now I need you to provide further information regarding your secret weapon."

Tesla did so (I cannot report the details), and then told us that he must leave for an appointment. "But before I do, there is one more thing I should like to know, Mr Holmes."

"And that is?"

"However did you know that I came to you because something was stolen from me?"

With a smile, Holmes answered, "You place me in the position of a magician who must tell his secrets. When he does, the inquirer is almost certainly disappointed. I promise to answer you at a later time, if only to preserve the mystery a bit longer."

Tesla accepted that and after shaking hands with us, our new client departed.

Once we were alone, I said that I could have answered Tesla's last question. "You learned that he was coming and why from your brother."

"True, Watson."

"Therefore you also know where to look for the stolen plans."

"I am afraid not. Mycroft is working on it, but encouraged me to do so as well."

I poured myself a cup of tepid tea. "This business is quite serious. You've told me—well, you practically threatened me about Moriarty."

"But fortunately, Watson, so far I have only crossed his path once—I think it was during that business of the Naval Treaty, though I could be mistaken—but though my efforts frustrated the professor, he does not realize that it was I who was responsible."

We later learned that this was one of the few times that Sherlock Holmes was mistaken.

The next morning, Holmes disguised himself as a brick-layer, but before setting out he found little Jimmy Stuart, one of the most reliable of the Baker Street Irregulars (the ragamuffins who serve as Holmes's secret eyes and ears).

"Master James," he said to the lad, "I want you to scour the landscape for any rumours of offers to sell plans for secret weapons."

"But, Mr 'Olmes," said Jimmy, "that's too big a job for me to do meself."

"Quite right. Gather any of the other Irregulars you require to assist."

The boy smiled. "Right-o, guv! We'll report back as soon as we can." And with that, he scampered off with more energy that I've had since I was a field doctor.

"Holmes, may I inquire where you are off to?"

"I have no idea." He left and I did not see him until the following morning, when he appeared, hungry and in need of a shave.

"Good morning, Holmes. Were your efforts successful?"

"Too much so, Watson. There are at least seventy-five secret weapons on the market."

Just then, in walked Jimmy. "Mr 'Olmes," he said, "we've found seventy-five weapons up for sale."

Holmes nodded. "So did I."

But when they compared their efforts, Holmes learned to his dismay that not one of Jimmy's seventy-five secrets were the same as the other group!

"This means," Holmes groaned, "that we must compare all one hundred and fifty."

They did so, and to our mutual relief, nearly all of them not only canceled each other out, but were clearly not Tesla's weapon. This left only three secrets for Holmes to investigate.

He devoted himself to that labour all day. When he was finished, it was about 6:30 in the evening and he made the first order of business a request to Mrs Hudson for dinner. Well, she'd been waiting for him to say so and quite patiently, I might add—I have no idea how!

Soon we sat down to a kingly feast: Lamb de Beauville, pota-toes amandine, spinach Sherwood (named for the forest), and for dessert, cherries and pineapple in rum.

As we relaxed over brandy and coffee, Holmes said, "This has been a frustrating day. I've learned nothing."

"Then what do you propose to do?"

"Visit my brother to begin with. But I am worried, Watson, quite worried."

"Indeed, yes. So am I. You must engage the professor a second time, and unlike your first encounter he may learn about you."

"Watson," he said somberly, "I've bad news. I was mistaken about that earlier contretemps. He knows that I was behind it. It is surprising that he took no action against me, but this time I will not be so lucky. Nor—"

He stopped himself, but I completed his thought. "He may also come after me and perhaps even Mrs Hudson."

He nodded. "I do not think he would bother with either of you, but the man is so unscrupulous, I cannot ignore the potential risks."

"I have a suggestion, Holmes. She has an uncle in Yorkshire and she says he has been ailing. Perhaps we could persuade her to pay him a visit, or better yet, travel to him as an errand of mercy."

"Excellent, Watson!" The very next morning, Mrs Hudson de-parted for the North. We went to the station to see her off (and to guard against any possible attack). As we rode off in a hansom toward Baker Street, Holmes said, "I'm relieved that that's taken care of. Now as for you—"

"As for Yours Truly, I shall not—never will!—quit your side. By now you should know that."

"I do, my dear Watson. I just needed to hear it once more." And without further regrets or qualms, he outlined what we were about to do. For a moment I wished I could rejoin my regiment wherever they be, no matter how bloody. It did seem like the more prudent course of action.

For what he expected of me was to perfect a German accent. Now I have a good ear for music but it does not extend to languag-es. But later that day he devoted himself to teach me and I began to feel like Eliza Doolittle. (No, that is inaccurate. I did not see Bernard Shaw's *Pygmalion* till quite a few years later). At length I was sufficiently schooled to feel confident (not much, though) that

I could pose as a German purchasing agent. Holmes had already placed a pertinent advertisement in several local newspapers.

Our answer came that very afternoon when little Jimmy Stuart arrived from Holmes's postal drop with a sealed envelope that he handed to the sleuth.

> Three billion marks, plus thirty per cent of all subsequent profits. If you are able to purchase the item in question, then come to the Porter's Rest on Fleet Street tomorrow at two p m. Approach the table under the German flag hanging on the wall.

Shortly after noon the following day we set out, somewhat early, I thought.

"Are you ready, Herr Obermann?"

"I certainly hope so."

But before going to Fleet Street, Holmes diverted us to the Diogenes Club. In the event that you have not read my remarks concerning Mycroft Holmes and the Diogenes Club, let me satisfy your curiosity. Mycroft is both older and smarter than Sherlock and this by Holmes's own admission. But the senior member of the clan is decidedly rotund and equally indolent. His daily rounds are from his home[2] to his offices in Whitehall and thence to the Diogenes. He has a governmental function that his sibling assures me is of paramount importance and he apparently never sloughs off his duties. But most of the time each day he is at his club, which caters to very private individuals. Only the visitor's room permits talking, but in all other parts of the club, speech is strictly forbidden!

It is important that you understand Mycroft Holmes's laziness. (Sherlock says his daily routine is as fixed as a planet's orbit.) For then you will realize why both Holmes and I were astonished to learn that he was not there.)

"I presume he is at work," Holmes said.

"Perhaps he has been summoned."

"No one summons my—wait, that is not true. Her Majesty could fetch him at a moment's notice, for she can find him even when I could not without considerable effort. If he was called for, then it would be a matter of national—perhaps international importance."

2   I am not at liberty to provide particulars. Indeed, I do not know them. But Holmes says that it would be easier to track down Queen Victoria at a secret retreat than Mycroft Holmes if he elected to disappear.

"Wouldn't Tesla's problem qualify?"

"Indeed it would."

Just then, the club's major-domo arrived, scant of breath. "Ah, Mr Sherlock." (I supposed he dared this familiarity by way of Mycroft) "I am so glad that you are still here." He proffered a folded scrap of paper, which Holmes accepted. "Your brother was certain that you would show up on the way to your appointment."

Holmes's brows shot up. "You know about that?"

"No, no, not at all! I was merely quoting your brother."

"Ah, of course." As the functionary gratefully retired, Holmes unfolded the missive, read it and then handed it to me. "This is interesting. See what you make of it, Watson."

Here is what I read—

> S—by all means tell the enemy that we shall meet any price.—M

"Obviously," I said, "he is prepared to commit our government to pay a considerable sum of money."

"True, but what else do you notice?"

"Well, your brother's handwriting is quite graceful."

"He studied penmanship. For that matter, so did I, but only as a tool in the interpretation of clues. Now focus on his words. What do you see now?"

I reread it several times. "I do note how economically he expresses himself."

"There, Watson…you have hit upon it."

"You mean that I'm right?"

He shook his head. "Sorry. You have found what I've been giving you grief about and that is something. This is the passage in question—'…tell the enemy we shall meet any price….'"

"That's what I said, Holmes. Ever so succinct."

"But not quite. Mycroft's laziness extends to language. All he need have said was, 'We shall meet any price.'"

At last I saw what he was driving at. "So by suggesting to 'tell the enemy,' et cetera, his true meaning is that we must lie to them."

"Precisely!"

When we finally arrived at our destination, I was surprised, and perhaps Holmes was, too, to find that only one man was seated at the table beneath the German flag. He looked vaguely familiar. He did not rise, but gestured for us to take seats opposite him.

"My name," he said, "is Isadora Persano. Perhaps you've heard of me?"

"Indeed, yes!" I exclaimed. "You are England's preeminent duellist."

He patted the cane that he gripped in one hand. "If you say so." He gestured to the bartender and that worthy stopped in mid-conversation and hurried over to our table.

"Another round for me, and take orders from these gentlemen, who are my guests."

The bartender ducked his head like the world's foremost toadie.

Holmes ordered a dry sherry, whilst I indulged myself with coffee and a single malt scotch (which was at that time a fairly new thing in London).

Said Holmes, "Allow me to introduce Major Blantyre. He has been empowered by the German government to purchase Mr Tesla's invention at the stipulated price."

Persano sipped his drink, then smiled coldly, reminding me of a serpent about to strike. "That is gratifying news, Mr Holmes."

"Who?" my friend sputtered. "You have me mistaken for someone else. I am merely a minor attaché sent here in case you and the Major require an interpreter."

Persano shook his head. "What you claim to be I might have credited, but my employer instructed me minutely on who I should expect to meet. Therefore, I repeat—Mr Holmes." He turned to me. "And you are, of course, Dr John H (for Hamish, I do believe) Watson, M D, late of an Indian regiment."

Holmes threw up his hands. "Well, you—or, rather, the professor—are on to us. We might as well go back to Baker Street."

And I had not even had an opportunity to try out my German accent!

Persano held up a forestalling hand. "My dear Mr Holmes, why do you think that you must give up? Do you have proof that you can meet the terms of our offer?"

Holmes sat back down again, smiling (which ought to have warned Persano). "As a matter of fact, I do have a missive here from my brother Mycroft." He offered the folded paper to him, which the duellist read it, then bestowed a decisive nod on us.

"You may not be aware, Dr Watson, that I always read and enjoy your accounts of Mr Holmes's adventures in *The Strand*. I recollect in one of them the information that at some times Mr Holmes's elder brother *is* the British government. In other words, we will happily return the object in question upon receipts of the necessary funds, which must be in small denominations.

"Because this will prove somewhat onerous, we will supply a brougham at our expense to carry the treasure. Will you meet us tomorrow in front of this establishment at, say, three in the afternoon? That should give you, or rather, Mr Mycroft Holmes, enough time to obtain the cash."

Holmes agreed and we left the place, hailed a cab and hurried off again to the Diogenes Club. This time, Mycroft Holmes was present.

"Particulars?" he asked.

"The entire sum must be delivered by three o'clock tomorrow," Holmes replied. "It must be in small denominations."

Mycroft rang for the major-domo, who swiftly supplied libations to our trio. After he was gone, Mycroft said, "Small denominations will be a nuisance but not impossible. I am concerned, though, about you both."

"Why?" I wondered, but Holmes—the younger one—answered me.

"Because when Moriarty does not receive his money, you and I, Watson, will be his targets."

A moment of troubled silence, and then Mycroft said, "That's understood. Now, gentlemen, here is what you must do."

The next day at three o'clock the exchange took place. We watched the brougham waddle off and then Holmes suggested that we take in an early concert at the Tivoli Hall, which we did. Afterward, we travelled some distance to dine together. We did not return to Baker Street till it was nearly ten at night.

Isadora Persano, fuming, was there to greet us.

"Holmes!" he snapped. "I should not have thought you capable of this!"

Holmes took off his cape and hat, poured glasses of wine for all of us and said, "This is an amontillado almost worth being walled up for." He took a sip, then added, "I have no idea why you are so upset. Watson and I have been attending a splendid concert—look, here are our programmes! I'd thought our business was concluded successfully."

Persano tasted his amontillado and his eyes widened appreciably.

"Gentlemen, my apologies…I have been too precipitate. But shortly after the brougham rode off, it was stopped by three masked men with pistols. They stole every last shilling!"

"I am quite upset to hear this," said Holmes. "After the concert, we dined and, as you see, have just returned. But if you don't mind waiting, I will immediately seek out my brother. It should not take long. While I'm gone, do have more wine or whatever else might appeal to you."

The duellist nodded. "I do feel rather peckish."

My friend rang for Mrs Hudson and asked her to accommodate our guest. Then he left us and I wondered what on earth we could do to pass the time, but Persano turned out to be a gifted conversationalist and as we shared Mrs H's "impromptu," we talked about everything from art and literature to politics and world history.

In less than an hour, Holmes was back. "I have some good news—well, not as good as you'd wish, yet better than you may have expected."

"Do tell!"

"Yes, Mr Persano, I will. It consists of two items. First, Mycroft not only already knew about the theft, he has identified its perpetrator. Have you heard of a thug who calls himself Jack Sheppard?"

I recognized the name, having read about him in *The Newgate Calendar*. Originally, he worked for Jonathan Wild, but then set out on his own, even stealing from Wild himself! That worthy, of course, "peached" on him and Sheppard was arrested and imprisoned in a maximum security cell, from which, however, he escaped.

"My employer is well aware of Sheppard," our guest replied. "The fool created his own criminal network and has been getting in our way too often. This clinches it—he shall be taught a lesson he will only need to learn once."

That bothered me.

Persano began to leave, but then stopped himself. "You said there were two items on your agenda?"

"Yes," said Holmes. "My brother offers to reimburse you for half of the amount that was taken."

"Excellent! As a matter of fact, our price was deliberately inflated, so we would gladly have been bargained down to half. I shall go tell my employer about this at once!" He hurried off.

"Holmes," I said, "how can you and Mycroft throw Sheppard to the wolves? Even though he is a criminal—"

"A criminal who has committed murder and worse. Don't be concerned, Watson. Moriarty already has formed his plans to eliminate his enemy."

The following afternoon, Mrs Hudson opened the door and in came a man bearing three gift-wrapped packages, two of which he bestowed upon Holmes and the other larger one on me.

"Mr Tesla," Holmes said, surprised, "to what do we owe the honour?"

"I recently visited your brother … his club is quite appealing! If I lived here, I should apply for membership. Anyway, he told me that you have recovered my plans."

"Yes, we have."

"He also said that you would not accept any fee for your services."

A nod. "I was working for the British government."

"So *do* open your presents!"

I let Holmes go first. The slightly bulkier one contained a new calabash pipe. "Ahh", my friend smiled, "some artists have depicted me as smoking one of these, whereas I always use a straight clay pipe. Now I can make their portraiture come true." He then opened the second package and promptly sniffed its contents. "Good heavens, Mr Tesla! This is one of the finest—and most expensive—pipe tobaccos in the world!"

"Do enjoy it, Mr Holmes."

"But you are opposed to smoking!"

"For myself, but I never impose my opinions on anyone else. Now, Dr Watson, what are you waiting for?"

I removed the gift paper and discovered a bottle of single malt scotch!

Tesla soon left. The balance of the afternoon was devoted to relaxation and enjoyment of our respective gifts. But just when we were about to retire for the evening, Isadora Persano returned. He had an envelope that he gave to Holmes, then said good night and departed.

Holmes opened the letter, read it and passed it to me.

> S—you must know that I saw right through this charade. You had very little to do with it. It positively reeks of your brother. But I let you stay out of it, for he was merely exercising his ego. His counter-offer is wholly acceptable. As long as you do not get in my way in future, there shall be no repercussions.—J M

I poured more scotch. But I was worried.

"Yes, Watson? Say it."

"I know you all too well, Holmes. You have no intention of leaving Moriarty alone."

A deep sigh. "Thanks to me, his entire organization is about to come crashing down. He will not be apprehended, though, for he has covered his tracks too well, as have both Persano and a certain former military man who I shall tell you about later."

I set down my glass. "Then sometime soon, you, myself, and Mrs H may expect severe retaliations?"

"I think it unlikely that he will bother either of you. No, I shall be his target, though perhaps Mrs Hudson, at least, should go on a long vacation. Ah, Watson, may I have a taste—?" I gestured for him to have some scotch.

"This is superb!" He exhaled and enjoyed its after-taste. "You see, my friend, Moriarty has climbed so high that it is inevitable that he must suffer a great fall. When that happens, I *do* intend to be there to witness it."

As it happened—with surprising celerity—Holmes's prediction came true.

I mean that quite literally.

✗

THE REVENGE OF THE FENIAN BROTHERHOOD

by Carole Buggé

Come all ye young rebels and list while I sing,
For the love of one's country is a terrible thing
It vanishes fear with the speed of a flame
And makes us all part of the Patriots's Game

—*Tommy Makem*

We have received many unusual visitors in our rooms on the second floor of 221 Baker Street, but I cannot remember any appearance more unexpected than that of the personage who appeared at our door on a cold, wet November night in 1889. I was, in fact, left speechless for some time—though Holmes, displaying his usual *sang froid*, calmly motioned our visitor towards the sofa.

"You realize, of course, my distaste in coming to you for assistance in this matter," said our caller, settling his thin, bony frame into the depths of the sofa.

"Naturally," Holmes replied, digging his long fingers into the Persian slipper which served as his tobacco tin.

I stood staring as foolishly as a school boy, until Holmes laid a hand gently on my shoulder.

"Please sit down, Watson; you are making me nervous."

I sat slowly in my usual chair in front of the crackling fire, never taking my eyes off our guest. I don't know what I thought he would do, but although I had never laid eyes on him before I was certain that this was a man you did not turn your back on.

Holmes was more sanguine, however, and deliberately turned his back to procure a match from the mantelpiece. At this our visitor chuckled.

"Always the showman, eh, Holmes?" he said in a low voice, hissing his s's, his grey eyes as hooded as a viper's. He turned his steely gaze on me, and it was then I first made eye contact with the late Professor James Moriarty.

"No more than yourself," Holmes replied, lighting his pipe and turning to face the Professor.

"Now it is you who are making me nervous, Holmes—sit down, please," I said, my eyes still trained on Moriarty; some instinct deep within me would not let me take my gaze off of him. I had always thought of him as the personification of evil, and yet now what struck me about his face was how deeply pain was etched into every line, every crevice—as though someone had taken a sharp knife and carved out a mask of suffering. His eyes were dead, though, as cold and lifeless as the lidless eyes of a fish.

Holmes sat in the winged armchair opposite mine. "Now, then, Professor, what can I do for you?"

Moriarty gave off a long, slow exhalation of breath, which made a low hissing sound like air escaping from a tyre. There was a long pause as he rose and walked to the window, pulling aside the curtains to look out on the street below. I tensed in my chair, ready to spring, my mind racing—it occurred to me that he might be giving a signal of some kind. I glanced at Holmes, who appeared utterly unconcerned; he sat smoking peacefully, his eyes half-closed, fingers folded in repose on his lap.

Finally Moriarty spoke. "What a pitiful sight mankind is," he said, still gazing out onto the street, "hurrying back and forth like so many ants, and all to what purpose? To work and spawn and die, with no more mindfulness than a doomed salmon swimming upstream towards his death."

"You certainly did not come here to philosophise with me," said Holmes. "May I ask—"

"You are unaware, perhaps that I have a brother?" Moriarty interrupted, swivelling to face us, and again I was struck by the pain which had hardened into the lines of his face.

"I had heard something of it," Holmes replied, "from my own brother."

"Ah, yes, Mycroft," Moriarty said, his thin lips curling into something resembling a smile.

"I believe he lives in Ireland, does he not?"

Again Moriarty sighed, but when he spoke his voice was a sneer. "If anyone could be said to actually 'live' in Ireland. He is, in fact, a Catholic priest."

If Holmes felt any surprise at this revelation he betrayed none. Moriarty, however, snickered. "Yes, it is ironic, isn't it? A brother who is a man of the cloth—when I have devoted myself to quite another kind of priesthood."

"He is in trouble, your brother?"

Moriarty nodded, his large head swivelling precariously on its long, thin neck; it was as though the head of a bull had been set upon the body of a giraffe.

"We had a—falling out, shall we say—and have not spoken for some years, and yet—when I came by the information that I am about to tell you I had no choice but to intervene."

"No choice—?"

Moriarty smiled, and though I would not say it was a warm smile, some of the hard lines on his face softened. "It may surprise you to know that even I have areas in my life which are—sacred, so to speak."

"Not at all," Holmes replied. "I would have assumed as much."

"I am afraid that it is so unoriginal as to be a cliché, but I made a promise to my dying mother that no matter what came I would look after my younger brother Sean. And I have kept that promise—until now, that is."

"I see; pray continue."

Moriarty walked back to sit upon the couch again; his gait swayed like that of a large flightless bird.

"You have perhaps heard of the Fenian Brotherhood?"

"I have heard of them, yes—they are essentially a terrorist organization bent on the eradication of British rule in Ireland. Is your brother mixed up with them?"

"On that contrary; he is their sworn enemy. I have reason to believe they have kidnapped him."

"I see." Holmes's face was stoic as ever, but he could not conceal the gleam of interest in his grey eyes, which burned dark as coals in the dull November light.

"So you see your involvement in this case would be for the good of England as well. If you don't believe me, ask your brother

Mycroft; he is privy to every bit of international intelligence, is he not?"

Holmes just smiled in reply. "Why do you come to me for assistance when you have a network of your own upon which to draw?"

Moriarty's face hardened again, and his dark eyes clouded over. "Because my brother must know nothing of my involvement in his rescue. He knows my agents, and he knows the way I operate. He has taken great pains to disassociate himself from me—"

"And yet you protect him—" I blurted out.

"As I said, Dr Watson, every man has some things that are sacred."

"Say no more," Holmes said graciously; "I see your predicament. Do you know whether Scotland Yard has been informed of this matter yet?"

Moriarty let out what could have been taken for a laugh—a short, brutal exhalation of air. "If they have, they have not learned it from me."

"Why don't you tell me what you know?"

"There isn't much to tell. My brother was invited to preach at a notoriously pro-Fenian church here in London, and his subject matter did not sit well with certain factions in the congregation... the next day he went out in the morning and did not return."

"I see. Naturally you suspect elements of that organization."

"Let's just say there's a strong certainty, Holmes." Moriarty's eyes narrowed and darkened. "It's well for them that I am not handling this myself...I would make them pay in ways you cannot imagine," he said in a cold, flat voice.

I shuddered at not so much his words as the way he said them.

Holmes rose from his chair. "I will begin working on it immediately."

Moriarty rose stiffly and walked to the door in his peculiar, swaying gait. When he reached the door he paused.

"You realize, of course, that this changes nothing between us?"

Holmes smiled. "Of course."

Their eyes met briefly and they exchanged a look extraordinary in its contradictions—it was full of understanding without friendship, admiration without affection; the sort of look two opposing generals might give one another on the eve of battle. Without another word Moriarty turned and was gone. I listened as his footsteps descended the stairs, and only when I heard the front door latch behind him did I turn to Holmes.

"I didn't know he had a brother."

Holmes shrugged. "Neither did I."

"But you said—"

"My dear Watson, with a man like Moriarty it is better not to admit ignorance on any matter if you can avoid it."

"But how did you know he lived in Ireland?"

"That was a lucky guess; Moriarty is an Irish name."

"But what if this whole thing is a trap?"

"I think we can rule that out easily enough," he replied, opening the door to the sitting room. To my surprise, our landlady Mrs Hudson was standing in the hallway outside. She wore an apron and there was flour on her hands.

"Yes, Mrs Hudson?" said Holmes with a smile.

"I just thought I'd come up and see…if everything was all right—that is," she said, flustered.

"Quite all right, thank you," Holmes replied, scribbling something on a piece of paper. "Would you see that Master Tuthill of the Baker Street Irregulars gets this?" he said, handing the note to Mrs Hudson.

"Yes, sir," she answered, tucking it into the pocket of her apron. "Mr Holmes, may I ask you something? That fellow who was just here…he—what I mean is, was he—?"

"Yes, Mrs Hudson, he was. And now don't let us detain you any longer; please return to your baking."

"What—? Oh, yes," she said, looking at her flour-covered hands. "Yes, of course…"

"Goodbye, Mrs Hudson, and thank you," Holmes said firmly.

"You're welcome, Mr Holmes; quite welcome, I'm sure." She looked as if she wanted to say something else, but Holmes escorted her gently to the door and closed it behind her.

"The less she knows about this the better for her," he said, heading for his bedroom.

"He's telling the truth, you think, then?"

"We shall find out soon enough. It's time for a visit to Brother Mycroft."

The Diogenes Club was in Pall Mall, across from Mycroft's rooms, and a short distance from his office. His routine rarely varied; he could be found in his office until precisely four forty-five, at which time he made his way to his club, then at exactly seven-forty trundled off to his lodgings. It is ironic that the physical universe inhabited by this extraordinary creature was as limited as his mental world was expansive. Holmes had once confided to me that Mycroft was not only his intellectual superior, but that "one might even say that Mycroft *is* the government." Holmes was not a man given to exaggeration, and so my respect for his brother Mycroft was considerable.

We entered the august edifice which housed the club, a heavy grey stone building typical of the mid-Victorian period, and headed straight for the Visitors' Lounge, the only room in the cavernous structure in which conversation was allowed. Mycroft Holmes was seated in an armchair, and I thought he had grown a tad heftier since our last encounter. His grey eyes were as keen as his brother's, however, and his massive skull was evidence of the same magnificent brain power. I sat—or rather sank—down upon a low overstuffed armchair.

"You are dealing with an offshoot of the Fenians called the Triangle," he said, without any conversational preamble. "They call themselves The Invincibles, or Clann na Gael. Some of their darker deeds include the murder of Lord Frederick Cavendish, shortly after he was appointed Chief Secretary for Ireland, in 1882; they are also suspected of crimes in the United States. They are ruthless and will stop at nothing to achieve their goal of Irish independence."

He paused and lit the pipe which sat at on the arm of his chair, and thin reeds of smoke curled around his broad head.

"The government has already received a ransom note in the matter of Moriarty's brother, offering to exchange him for Fenian prisoners. An exchange is of course out of the question. The men we hold are directly implicated in the dynamite campaign of 1883, in which a number of bombs were set off all over England, some of which killed innocent people."

"One more thing," said Mycroft as we rose to leave; "we have reason to believe that a bomb will be planted in a major edifice somewhere in London within the next few days. I needn't tell you that the consequences could be catastrophic." He handed Holmes a piece of paper. "These password phrases may or may not work; however, it is the most current information we have."

"I see," said Holmes. He studied the paper, his lean face tight, his grey eyes gleaming in the dim light of the Diogenes Club.

Mycroft walked us to the door, and as we turned to leave he laid a hand on his brother's shoulder.

"Be careful, Sherlock."

I was struck more by the uncharacteristic gesture than by his words, but Holmes just nodded.

Outside, we stood for a moment watching a dimly glimmering twilight settle over London. Holmes stood upon the stairs, his sharp profile silhouetted against the waning light in the western sky. I wondered what thoughts were racing through that quicksilver brain when suddenly he shook off his mood, sprang into the street, and hailed a cab. The cab ride back to Baker Street was spent in silence; Holmes sat in the corner wrapped in thought, and I knew better than to disturb him at times like this.

When we arrived at Baker Street Holmes went straight to his bedroom without a word. I sat down on the couch and filled my pipe. I didn't like this, any of it, but I was so accustomed to deferring to Holmes in most matters that I didn't know if I should say anything. My concern turned to astonishment a few minutes later when Holmes emerged from the bedroom dressed in a black suit and clerical collar.

"What do you think, Watson?"

"Good heavens, Holmes!"

"I admit it's a bit of a stretch, but it's necessary under the circumstances."

"But—"

"Oh, I know; my soul could go straight to hell."

"I didn't mean that, but don't you think it's a bit—"

"Sacrilegious? I suppose it is, but I'm sure I've committed worse sins. And now if you'll excuse me, I shall be off," he said, throwing his black Ulster on over his priestly garb. "Tell Mrs Hudson I shall be back in time for dinner and that I look forward to the fine fruit tart she is preparing for us."

I didn't even bother to ask Holmes how he knew it was a fruit tart. I closed the door after him and wandered around the sitting room for a while, trying to make sense of the strange events of the morning. Finally I lay down upon the couch and attempted to immerse myself in some medical texts which I had recently purchased. My mind was having none of it, however, and soon I drifted off into uneasy dreams in which masked gunmen tried to pull me off the couch where I lay. I clung to my pillow, though, until I heard Mrs Hudson's voice coming from one of the gunmen.

"Dr Watson, wake up! There's a message for you."

I sat up abruptly and took the slip of paper which she held in her hand. I opened it and read:

"Meet me at Paddy O'Reilly's—Holmes. P S…bring your revolver."

"Thank you, Mrs Hudson." I rose from the couch, groggy from the sleep which still clung to me. I thrust the note into my pocket and, with trembling hands, took my service revolver from the desk drawer and loaded it.

"I'm going out, Mrs Hudson," I said, smoothing my hair and buttoning my cuffs. My wife had just given me a beautiful new pair of gold cufflinks with my initials engraved on them, and I was very taken with them.

"Wouldn't you like some tea before you leave?" she said, picking up the sofa pillows which I had flung about the room in my dream-tossed slumber.

"No, thank you—I haven't any time."

As I closed the door behind me, she was fussing about the room muttering something about "regular hours" and "all this dashing about."

The weather had cleared, and a brisk wind had picked up from the river. I pulled my coat about me as I stood waiting for a cab to arrive; and soon I was seated in a hansom rumbling east along the cobblestones.

London's East End is sometimes referred to as "the other London." This catch-all description includes the opium dens and whore houses in neighborhoods such as Whitehall and Spitalfields; it also describes the colorful but less ominous environs which respectable working class English people and foreigners made their home. The men and women who cleaned the houses and chimneys of the richer folk, who shod their horses and shined their shoes, who baked their pastries and sewed their clothes—these hardworking people resided to a large extent in the Eastern sector of the city. Holmes and I had often journeyed into these places—as a source of information, the pubs and tea rooms of the East End were invaluable. The Irish pubs of Spitalfields were no exception. In London in 1891 an Irishman was regarded as closer to a foreigner than an Englishman. They retaliated by taking their business en masse to the East End.

An Irish pub is not like an English pub. It is noisier, more bois-terous, and more vital. There is usually music, there is often danc-ing, and there is always drinking—not polite social drinking, but serious, determined drinking, the consumption of alcohol serving as a revolt against the insults of the world. I am half Irish myself, and as a child I saw what motivated that kind of drinking, and also what it could do to a man.

Paddy O'Reilly's was the kind of place you could go to forget the insults of the world—to drown them in a glass of stout if that was your choice—or to lose them in a reel played hard and fast on a concertina and a tin whistle. The sound of the music reached me even before I put my hand upon the handle of the heavy oaken door. It was a tune I recognized—"Mary's Wedding," a Scottish melody, and it was being played at breakneck speed on a fiddle and concertina, with a tin whistle supplying a kind of obligator or counterpoint. I stood in the doorway for a moment, pushed back by the harsh smell of tobacco, sawdust, and beer. The concertina player was middle-aged, with the heavy-lidded eyes of a Scots-man, and he sat pumping his instrument with a grim determination. Four or five dancers stomped out something close to the Highland fling, and a few other people watched them, clapping and laughing with a bleary-eyed euphoria.

I made my way across the sawdust-strewn floor, heading for a lone figure sitting hunched over at a table at the back of the room. I was very nearly drawn into the dance by a raucous young woman who attempted to link her arm around mine. Her red hair was wild; her eyes were wilder, and I extracted myself from her clutches, mumbling a polite excuse, and made my way to the back of the room.

When I reached the solitary man, who was seated at a dimly lit table in the corner, I sat down. When I looked at his face I thought I had made a mistake; surely the ruddy complexion and full cheeks did not belong to my friend Holmes. I began to rise, but I felt a strong hand upon my should pull my back down.

"Sit still, Watson! Do you want to call attention to us?"

It was unmistakably Holmes's voice, and I could not prevent the look of astonishment which crossed my face.

"Holmes!" I whispered, "it *is* you, then!"

"Of course it is. Now keep still and try not to look suspicious."

Holmes ordered two glasses of stout from the surly waiter, whose cigarette perched upon his lower lip, defying the laws of gravity and physics.

"Try to look inconspicuous," Holmes muttered as the man set two foaming mugs in front of us.

"By the way, what happened to your last disguise?" I said, taking a sip of the heavy, sweet dark liquid in my glass.

"It was very useful for a time." He smiled. "I'm afraid I violated the sanctity of the confessional, but as you know, Watson, I am not religious."

"You mean—you posed as a priest to hear confessions?"

"The Fenians are Catholics to a man, and a Catholic may do any number of heinous deeds, but if he is a good Catholic he will always confess it to his priest."

"Holmes—!" I was raised Church of England myself, but still I admit I was shocked.

"Yes, Watson; no doubt I am a sinner, and if there is a hell, I shall end up there." He dismissed the thought with a wave of his hand. "No matter; I now know the identity of at least one of the conspirators. You see that man there?" he said, indicating a large, heavy-shouldered man who stood watching the dancers as they spun and bobbed to the music. With his thick unruly hair and massive torso, he resembled a large brown bear.

"Yes?"

"He is a good Catholic; he is also a kidnapper, and very probably a murderer."

Just then, as if he had sensed we were talking about him, the man turned towards us, and I saw his lips part to reveal a mouth of large, yellowed teeth. His face was heavy and thick-featured, a crudely sensual face, and I shuddered at the sight of so many teeth set between those thick lips. His eyes moved about the room but did not settle upon us, and when he turned back to watch the dancers I exhaled heavily; I had been holding my breath.

"So you—you followed him here?" I whispered to Holmes.

"Yes, and it was no easy feat, let me tell you. A priest attracts more attention on the street than an ordinary man, and several times I had to dart behind buildings to make certain he didn't see me. But when he went in here I had some time to apply the makeup which you see I now wear."

I shook my head; there seemed to be no end to my friend's ingenuity.

"So what do we do next?" I asked, but just then Holmes's hand gripped my arm.

"Shhh—it is time!" he said in a low voice.

Our massive friend was now bending over a table full of men, a serious expression on his florid face. The others at the table were a grim-looking lot, and a tall, sallow man who appeared to be the leader was speaking, his head lowered; all the others listened to him intently. "Time for what?" I whispered to Holmes.

"The thing we have come here to see. Avert your gaze; don't let them see you looking at them!" Holmes hissed as one of the men at the table let his eyes roam idly around the room. It was too late, however; our eyes met and he nodded to me. His face would have been handsome except for his deeply pockmarked skin; his eyes were large and lustrous, and the high cheekbones bespoke an aristocratic heritage. My skin chilled as he bent over and said something to the thin sallow leader, who nodded and looked over at us.

"You have your revolver?" Holmes whispered.

"Right here in my pocket." I closed my fingers over the handle of the gun; the cool smooth metal was reassuring in my hand.

The pockmarked man straightened up and walked towards us, and my fingers tightened around the revolver. However, when he reached us he smiled.

"Are you finding it unusually warm in here?" he said in a cultivated, educated voice with just a trace of an Irish accent.

"The weather can be unpredictable this time of year," Holmes replied smoothly.

The man nodded, then turned and walked back to his table; once again he leaned over for a consultation with his leader. I held my breath; this was evidently the password which Mycroft had referred to, but he had said he was not certain if it would work. To my surprise, the man motioned to us, whereupon Holmes rose and walked over to the other table. I followed him, and I could feel the men's eyes on us but I tried to look unconcerned. I am not the actor Holmes is, though, and I am afraid I did not manage to look any more nonchalant than I felt. In truth, my heart was racing and my palms were oozing sweat. I have been under fire in wartime and managed to remain rather cool, but there was something in the stares of these men which sent tingling threads of fear up my spine.

The thin sallow man regarded us through half-closed eyes; he reminded me of a long yellow cat.

"I understand you are interested in the current climate," he said.

"My brother usually knows when it's going to rain," Holmes replied calmly.

The sallow man nodded, and motioned to his pockmarked lieutenant, who indicated that we should follow him. He led us across the sawdust-strewn floor, behind the musicians and other patrons, and through a narrow door on the other side of the bar. We followed him down a set of steep steps to a dimly-lit basement room. A few chairs were scattered about the room, and a podium stood underneath a flag of Ireland which had been tacked up on one wall.

"Wait here," he said, and with that, left us and went back upstairs. Holmes and I stood listening to the sounds coming from upstairs. Someone was singing in a faltering tenor:

> Oh Danny Boy, the pipes, the pipes are calling
> From glen to glen and down the mountainside

I wondered what we were waiting for, and was about to ask Holmes what was going on, but just then I heard the sound of footsteps upon the stairs. Our pockmarked friend reappeared, followed by the large, thick-lipped fellow we had seen earlier, as well as the sallow man whom I took to be the leader. The rest of the men in his entourage were close behind, as well as a few others which I supposed had been scattered among the pub patrons. I estimated that there were perhaps two dozen people in the room including ourselves.

To my surprise, the wild-haired redhead was also among them, the only woman in the group. Holmes and I took our seats among the other patrons, and as we did, the young woman caught my eye and smiled. Though I averted my gaze, she came and sat next to us, brushing my leg with her long skirt as she did so.

"And what might your name be?" she said in a voice somewhat the worse for whiskey.

"Uh…Hugo," I said uncertainly.

"Oh, are you French, then?"

I looked at Holmes, but he sat staring straight ahead.

"On my mother's side."

"Oh, the French are very romantic, aren't they?" she replied, snuggling up closer to me.

"I—I don't know," I said miserably.

"Oh, but you should know…I could teach you, you know."

Just then our pockmarked friend banged a gavel upon the podium at the front of the room.

"All right, it's time we began," he said, and the room quieted down. "Let's all listen to what Brother Kerry has to say."

The wan-faced leader took the podium. He stood for a moment gazing at his audience and then he spoke.

"Our fight has just begun. As most of you know, we are ready to strike a blow which will leave our English oppressors reeling. I will let Brother O'Malley tell you about it."

With that, he stepped away from the podium and allowed the pockmarked man to take his place.

"This is the grandest plan we have ever conceived," Brother O'Malley began, but just then the intoxicated young woman grasped my hand in hers. I pulled away, but her grip was tight, and as I pulled back the cufflink on my right sleeve came off and fell to the floor. She bent down and picked it up, and then her eyes fell upon the engraved initials: "JW."

"You said your name was Hugo," she said in a loud voice. Brother O'Malley stopped midsentence and looked at us.

"Is there a problem?" he said in a stern voice.

To my horror, the young woman stood up, swaying uncertainly.

"Yes, Annie; what is it?" Brother O'Malley said impatiently.

"We have a spy among us," she said, pointing at me. At that moment my blood froze and ran cold in my veins; I felt as if the floor had suddenly been removed out from under me.

"Oh?" replied O'Malley in a wary voice. "What makes you think that?"

By now everyone was looking at us. I looked at Holmes; he sat utterly still, his face impassive, barely breathing.

"This cuff link!" Annie declared, holding it up for all to see.

"What about it?" said Brother Kerry, a gleam of suspicion in his eyes.

"Well, he told me his name was Hugo, but his cuff links have the initials "JW"! I say he's a spy!"

There was a murmur of voices in the room. I slipped my hand into my pocket and gripped the revolver.

"Hmmm," said Brother O'Malley, and he walked slowly towards us. I cursed myself for having worn these cufflinks, and for having the misfortune to attract the attention of the inebriated young woman.

It was too late, however; I think Holmes also knew the gig was up, because he stood up when O'Malley reached us.

"How did you manage to procure our password?" said O'Malley.

Holmes shrugged and did not reply. O'Malley nodded to the large bear-like fellow, who was looming nearby. To my horror, the huge fellow took two steps towards Holmes and suddenly rammed his massive fist into my friend's stomach. Holmes groaned and fell to the floor. I drew my gun, but with a quickness I would not have given him credit for, the giant flicked his hand out with lightning speed and delivered a crushing blow to my wrist, sending the gun flying. Cradling my wrist in my other hand, I dropped to the floor.

"We don't take too kindly to spies, you know," said Brother O'Malley in a flat voice. He bent over Holmes, who lay gasping for breath.

"Who sent you?"

Holmes shook his head. O'Malley shrugged and turned to me. "Perhaps you will tell me—or it will not go well for your friend here." He motioned to the bear-like man again, and before I could stop him he kicked Holmes in the ribs. Holmes moaned and lost consciousness.

Just then Annie interposed herself between O'Malley and us.

"Stop it—stop it, I say!" she screamed, clawing at him wildly. O'Malley nodded to his goon, whereupon the man lifted her off her feet and carried her from the room.

"I always said women should not be allowed to be a part of this," muttered Brother Kerry, walking over to us.

"What shall we do with them?" said O'Malley.

"Oh, I think we can put them with our other friend for the time being—at least until we finish our meeting," he replied, looking down at Holmes. "He's no good to us right now, anyway."

O'Malley nodded to several of the men, whereupon I found myself being half-carried and half-dragged from the room. Several of the men followed behind, carrying Holmes. A blindfold was placed over my eyes, and abruptly locked into darkness, I experienced the sensations which I imagined a blind man must feel. My world consisted now only of my other four senses, and I was suddenly very aware of the sounds and smells around me. I heard the smooth voice of O'Malley faded into the background and was replaced by the heavy steps of my captors, whose labored breathing indicated that they were unused to such strenuous exercise.

I was carried along for some ten minutes, and then I heard the high-pitched cry of seagulls and smelled the thick brackish aroma of the Thames; we were near the river. A door was opened and we entered a room; then another door, and then we stopped. I was shoved rudely into a chair, and I felt my hands and feet being tied. Then the blindfold was removed, and when my vision cleared I saw that I was in a long, low-ceilinged room, the walls and floor entirely made out of crude wooden planks; the kind of room you would see in a warehouse by the docks. Buoys and rusted anchors hung from the walls; coils of rotted rope sat in corners gathering dust; the warehouse had evidently been abandoned for some time. The room smelled of mildew and salt water.

The massive fellow, whom his comrades addressed as Connors, was engaged in tying Holmes to a chair. O'Malley stood, arms folded, gazing out of a small window at the other end of the room, the pale light highlighting the craters on his face. It was then I noticed there was a third figure in the room: along the far wall, in the shadows, I could barely make out the form of a man upon the floor, sitting slumped up against the wall. I strained my eyes to see better, but just then O'Malley turned and spoke.

"You stay and stand guard outside, Connors; we'll deal with them later," he said; "I have to get back to the meeting. Well, gentlemen," he continued, addressing himself to me, "I trust you will introduce yourselves to each other; I shall return as soon as I can."

With that he turned smoothly and left the room, followed by the other two men who had helped carry us here. Connors looked around the room, grunted, and then left. When he had gone I heard a bolt slide into place from the outside. Shortly afterwards I smelled cheap shag tobacco, and surmised that Connors was passing the time by having a smoke. I turned my attention to Holmes, who had begun to stir. My wrist had begun to throb, but I was far more concerned about his injuries than mine.

"Holmes—are you all right?" I whispered, not wanting Connors to hear our conversation. A moment passed, and then he replied in a weak voice.

"I'm all right, Watson—I was just stunned, that's all."

I didn't tell him that I suspected he had a broken rib or two. Instead I strained to make out the man in the corner. "Holmes, there's someone else in here with us!"

"Really?"

"Yes, over there in the corner!"

He twisted around to see, a move which caused him to wince in pain.

"Who is it, do you think?"

"I don't know; he looks as though he's been drugged, though."

"Yes, I expect you're right. Holmes—do you suppose it's— could it be—?"

"That would be the most logical conclusion, certainly."

Just then the man stirred and moaned softly.

"Hello—I say—hello there!" I whispered as loudly as I could.

He stirred again, and lifted his head. To my surprise, he chuckled softly.

"Well, well…Sherlock Holmes and Dr Watson, fancy meeting you here. I thought my brother might send you to rescue me."

"So you *are*—"

"Father Sean Moriarty, at your service," he said in a voice which had the same sibilant softness as his brother's but without the restrained violence underneath. "I am correct, however, in surmising that you are here at the behest of my brother?"

"Your brother and I are enemies," Holmes said evasively; "we are here on behalf of the British government."

"Very well, have it your way," Sean Moriarty said with a sigh. "I know he does not wish me to know of his involvement."

"What is important is not why we are here, but how we are going to get out of here," Holmes replied. "Are you able-bodied?"

"You were correct in surmising that I have been drugged, but the effect is now largely worn off; I thought it best to pretend I was still unconscious when our friends were here earlier."

"Good," said Holmes, and I mused that craftiness seemed to be one trait which remained consistent in both brothers.

"If they are going to kill us, they will not do so for at least one hour," Sean Moriarty continued.

"Why is that?" I said, my tongue going dry at his words.

"Because high tide is an hour away, and that is by far the best time to dispose of bodies; the outgoing tide would sweep them out toward sea."

"Admirably reasoned," said Holmes, and I felt a pang of jealousy at the approval in his voice.

"There's more at stake than just us, too," our fellow prisoner continued; "I overheard them plotting something else, something big involving a bomb."

There was a silence between us. I had already tried to work free of my bonds, but had only succeeded in giving myself rope burns; we were very securely and professionally bound.

We were evidently near one of London's busier docks, because I could hear the cries of costermongers outside, advertising their wares.

"Pickled eels—fresh, oy!"

"Get your cress, fresh watercress—penny a bunch!"

Holmes was listening, too, and even in the dim light I could see the muscles of his face working. Suddenly he pursed his lips and emitted a low, soft whistle. He paused and listened for a reply, and to my surprise it came almost at once, the same exact whistle! Holmes whistled again, this time repeating the same tone in short, staccato bursts. Again the answer came, and again Holmes replied. I was wondering where this was all leading when I saw a face appear at the window. It was a weathered, wizened face, with broken veins on the cheeks and a nose red from drink, but never in my life was I so glad to see a face!

Holmes nodded to the man, who nodded and then disappeared from view. A moment later there was sound of glass being cut, and I saw that the sound was being made by a thin blade inserted between the pane and the window frame. The three of us in the room held our breath as the glass was cleanly and skillfully separated from its base. Moments later another face reappeared, followed by a body. This time I recognized the face: it was Master Tuthill of the Baker Street Irregulars. The boy wriggled his thin form through the window, dropping noiselessly to the floor; then he crept over began untying us one by one. He had just started to untie me when the door was flung open and Connors's enormous bulk filled up the door frame.

"What's going on here?" he said. Before he could make a move, Holmes sprang at him, knocking him backwards through the door. His strength was enormous, though, and he flung Holmes off as easily as if he were a rag. Holmes staggered and then went at him again, landing several blows to the big man's torso. Connors grunted and struck out, but Holmes was lighter and quicker than his opponent, and easily avoided his blows.

"Hurry, Tuthill!" I cried as the boy struggled with my bonds.

"I'm goin' as fast as I can!"

Holmes was aiming his punches to Connors's face now, and the huge fellow was beginning to slow down when suddenly Holmes tripped over a coil of rotting rope. Connors took advantage of this and swung with all his might, and landed a blow to Holmes' ribs, whereupon my friend doubled over and slumped to the floor.

Free now from my restraints, I threw myself at Connors with a roar, but didn't even get near him; a blow to my head from one huge fist made me dizzy and I crumpled to the ground. My head spinning, I looked up through a haze of pain and saw Sean Moriarty rush at the big man. I closed my eyes, not wanting to see the results, but when I opened them moments later I saw Connors stretched out on the floor. Moriarty was standing over him, breathing heavily, rubbing his knuckles. I staggered unsteadily to my feet.

"Good Lord—what did you do to him?" I gasped.

"I did a bit of boxing before I was called to the priesthood," he replied modestly, and I stared at him in wonder. Though possessed of the same wiry frame as his brother, I would not have thought he could deck the big man like that. Tuthill stood looking at Moriarty with an expression of adoration.

I turned my attention to Holmes, who lay upon the floor looking very wan; I feared his injuries were causing internal bleeding.

"Dr Watson, how are you at knots?"

"I'm excellent, sir," Tuthill piped up; "I've worked on ship-board."

Moriarty regarded the lad. "Good," he said, pointing to Connors; "see that you tie him up well."

"Yes, *sir*!" said the boy, and grabbing one of the ropes formerly used on us, he set to work.

"We must get out of here before he comes to and tells the others," Moriarty said sharply, and then he bent over Holmes.

"Can you move?"

Holmes nodded, and we helped him to his feet. Gripping his side, his face deathly pale, he spoke in a raspy whisper. "What can you tell me—about what they—are planning?" he said, pausing between words to catch his breath.

I felt strongly that moving him was not a good idea, and yet we could not leave him here.

"I remember they said something about 'the third time's the charm'—"

"What else did they say? Can you remember anything else?"

"It's difficult; I was drugged at the time..." Moriarty paused, and then his face lit up.."Wait a minute—yes, they say something about 'the bird will have flown for the last time!'"

"Excellent!" cried Holmes, and then he winced and paused for breath. "Quickly, we must hurry!"

"Where are we going?" I said, following him out of the ware-house.

"To St. Paul's Cathedral!"

I immediately grasped Holmes's reasoning. Twice destroyed by fire, a bombing of St Paul's would indeed be "a third time." The 'bird' was a thinly veiled reference to Christopher Wren, the architect who designed the current building.

"May I come along, Mr Holmes?" said Tuthill.

"No, Tuthill, it could be very dangerous," Holmes replied; "but you have rendered us a great service today which I won't forget." The boy's beaming face showed the impact Holmes' praise had on him, and again I felt myself foolishly wishing those words had been spoken to me.

The night was dark and overcast but as the three of us scrambled up the bank of mud which led away from the river I could see the sweat gleaming on Holmes' forehead. When we reached Cannon Street we flagged down a cab.

"There's an extra guinea for you if you hurry!" Holmes cried to the driver, and soon we were rattling along the cobblestones at a brisk canter. The driver earned his money, for we arrived there within minutes.

St Paul's Cathedral's reputation as one of the greatest cathedrals in Europe is well deserved. Its dome dominates the skyline of the City like a mountain rising majestically out of foothills. Christopher Wren's design displays a harmony and balance which is both calming and exhilarating, and as we dashed through the marbled entryway I couldn't help feeling overwhelmed by its grandeur.

Suddenly Holmes gripped my arm. "There—there he is!"

I followed his gaze and saw the thin form of O'Malley dart behind a column.

"He's seen us," said Moriarty.

"Go around the back way, Watson; Moriarty and I will separate and cover the entrances."

I nodded and crept around the row of silent marble columns, my eyes straining to catch a sight of our quarry. The smooth floor and resonance of the walls made it difficult to move quietly, but I tiptoed as softly as I could. I stopped and listened. There was no sound except my own breathing, and I listened vainly for the echo of other footsteps.

Suddenly my eye caught a movement behind one of the columns. I froze and stopped breathing for what seemed like an eternity, then crept slowly forward.

"Well, Dr Watson, I must congratulate you—I don't know how you escaped, but now you will die a glorious death for the cause of Ireland."

I spun around to see O'Malley holding a gun pointed at my chest. Under his arm he carried an ominous-looking package wrapped in brown paper.

"Don't do it, O'Malley; think of the loss."

"Oh, but we're all thinking about loss all the time," he replied, his dark eyes narrow. "The loss of our homeland—the Ireland that once was but is no more thanks to the British government."

"But this won't solve anything," I said desperately; "you'll only be killing innocent people."

O'Malley shrugged. "Do you know how many people died in the potato famine because of the greed and indifference of British landlords? An eye for an eye. It's in the Bible, you know."

"And a tooth for a tooth."

O'Malley turned around to face Holmes, who stood there looking as pale as a ghost. As he did I threw myself at him, knocking him to the ground. I grabbed for the gun, and we fought for possession of it—then suddenly a shot rang out. O'Malley's eyes stared wildly into mine, and then his body went limp.

"Watson—are you all right?" Holmes cried, sinking to the ground beside us.

"Quite all right, thank you," I said, secretly pleased at the desperation in his voice. He was not a man given to emotional outburst, and it warmed me to the core to hear the concern he felt for my safety.

"Thank God," he said, and then gingerly picked up the package from where it had fallen on the floor. We opened it, and found that the timing device had not yet been set. "I think we'd best take this to Scotland Yard," he said as Sean Moriarty joined us. The commotion caused by the gunshot had already attracted several policemen, and I convinced Holmes to give them custody of the bomb and go back with me to Baker Street.

Only once we were safely back in our sitting room did I get a close look at Father Sean Moriarty. He had the same high domed forehead, the same thin lips as his brother, but without the cruelty about his mouth. His black eyes were softer, and as he sipped the tea which Mrs Hudson insisted on serving us, he shook his head, reminding me of the strange reptilian head swivelling which was peculiar to James Moriarty.

"My brother must have felt a bitter humiliation when he came to you for help." At Moriarty's insistence, Holmes and I both had finally stopped denying the involvement of James Moriarty.

I wanted to ask him how he and his brother had ended up at such different ends of the moral spectrum, but I contented myself with a question for Holmes, who lay on the couch at my insistence; after much protest, he had allowed my to bandage his ribs and administer some morphine.

"How did you know that they would take us to Father Moriarty if we were taken prisoner?"

Holmes stared at me for a moment and then let out a laugh, which caused him to wince and hold his side.

"Good Lord, Watson—you actually thought I *planned* to have us captured?"

"Well, didn't you?" said Moriarty.

"Good heavens, no; I was just there to infiltrate their meeting. Everything which happened afterwards was a complete surprise to me."

"But how did you know Tuthill was outside the window?" I said.

"I didn't; but I you may remember I sent him a note earlier. In it I just suggested that he keep an eye on our movements. He occasionally works as a costermonger's assistant, and as you can see, he did a good job of tracking us." Holmes smiled. "Well, Watson, I'd rather you didn't write this one up—I was employed by Professor Moriarty, nearly failed to prevent the destruction of St Paul's, and I was rescued by a priest and a little boy. Not a very successful case, I think, Watson."

"The public might enjoy knowing you are human after all, Holmes."

Holmes stretched and turned his face toward the pale light of dawn which was creeping through the curtains. "I think not, Watson; if they knew I was human, why on earth would they want to read about me?"

I smiled. "There are things in heaven and earth not dreamt of in your philosophy, Holmes."

Holmes shrugged. "Perhaps you are right, Watson; perhaps you are right."

THE THIRD SEQUENCE

By Sherlock Holmes

Edited by Bruce Kilstein

"*Spiritualism* has been so befouled by wicked charlatans, and so cheapened by many a sad incident, that one could almost wish that some such term as *psychic religion* would clear the subject of old prejudices, just as mesmerism…was rapidly accepted when its name was changed to hypnotism."

—Sir Arthur Conan Doyle
The Vital Message

Of the myriad cases which have come before me, there are many that have gone unsolved. The readers of my dear friend, John Watson's, accounts of so-called *adventures* have come to expect, sadly I must admit, a tidy conclusion to each investigation that I have undertaken wherein some dark business is exposed to the light of Justice. *Lux et Lex*. Watson's publications are pleasing enough; yet his tales with satisfying endings often give short-shift to the elucidation of the *process* of deductive reasoning which I employ in the prosecution of any inquiry. What would seem at once baffling to the careless eye of the police force may become a mere ordering of minutely observed facts with the exclusion of theories of the impossible.

Of all the places to which our inquiries have led us, from the most rancid opium den to the luxury of royal palaces, no corner has been so darkly impregnable than that of the human mind. The question of the motivations, the manipulations of the spirit that impel some to commit the basest of acts (not to mention the ease in which the victims are willing to be manipulated) continues to elude the best investigators. I am confident that science, in spite of the stunning advances of the last century, will continue to struggle to bring to light the forces that drive the engines of inhumanity. One has only to examine the suffering imposed by the Great War to realize that as a civilization we have not scratched the surface of what lies deep in the recesses of the human condition.

And so, I relate a tale that Watson has avoided disclosing. Suffice it to say that the lover of the mystery story may be intrigued but the reader seeking a simple explanation to events had best turn away.

It was in the autumn of 191_, the bees I had been studying had gone into dormancy, the skies had become sere and the ashen pall that covered the sensibilities of all Europeans had yet to be lifted in the aftermath of war. Perhaps with the prospect of a cold, inactive winter, I read with interest an article in the morning *Times*:

SPIRITUALIST MEDIUM ARRESTED
ON CHARGES OF MURDER!
Confessions linked to the ghostly realm.

London—In a grisly display, renowned psychic medium, M Marcel, was found by servants in the presence of three dead clients of his *séance* conducted the previous evening. The victims of foul play at Spivey House included Lady Regina Spivey and Colonel Jonathan Mills. Inspector Lestrade of Scotland Yard would offer no identity of the third deceased, citing matters of **National Security**, but is confident that the medium used his mesmeric influence to inflict harm upon his victims.

"What rubbish!" I muttered, tossing the paper to the floor. I summoned my housekeeper, Miss Finch, and instructed her to send telegrams to Watson and Mrs Hudson of my plans to travel to London. I penned the notes and consulted my Bradshaw's. "Tell the coachman I would like to make the 8:15 train to Victoria."

"Yes, Mr Holmes," she said. "You could use the telephone. It might be…"

"…a buzzing hive of eavesdroppers and gossips. Thank you, no, Miss Finch."

The sight of my Baker Street apartments, the rose glow of the fire and the familiar countenances of my friends served to dispel the melancholy which I had been experiencing.

"Holmes, what a surprise, old man! Let me help you with your case." Watson shook my hand vigorously and led the way into my old room.

"Wipe your feet, both of you," was Mrs Hudson's greeting as she finished beating dust from the sofa cushions before limping away rheumatically to fetch the tea.

I selected a pipe from the rack, scraped the Persian slipper for usable tobacco, and took stock of my aging colleague. "You look fit, Watson."

Watson chuckled. "Put on a few stone. Married life, you know. But, I must confess, I am shocked to see you here on such short notice. What could possibly be of such urgent…?"

Before he could finish, the brash voice and tread of Inspector Lestrade assaulted our senses. "…no need, I'll show myself in, Mrs Hudson." He burst into the room in a sodden Macintosh, paused, and realizing the impending brunt of our housekeeper's wrath, returned to the hall and hung the damp garment on the stand. "Well, Mr Holmes, I am delighted you have returned to London, no doubt to congratulate me on my most recent arrest."

Mrs Hudson brought the tea, frowning at the pool of water collected in the doorway as we gathered at the table.

"Quite, Lestrade," said I. "You have certainly outdone yourself this time. Pray, partake of the tea and enlighten the doctor and me on the particulars of this extraordinary act." I trusted that the Inspector could not resist the opportunity to sound his own horn. Watson took up a plate of cakes and I lit my pipe and closed my eyes, welcoming the sounds of the old house, the repast, the smell of tobacco and dust and, I must admit, even the shrill tenor of Lestrade's voice was a balm to my ears.

"A wonder, really," Lestrade began, between sips from his cup. "Three found dead and one in hospital from the doings at Spivey House two days ago. The group had gathered for some silly séance."

"I have heard of these gatherings," Watson said, the sound of brushing crumbs from his vest. "My friend, Dr Conan Doyle, is a strong believer and investigator of spirit phenomena. Strange stuff, if you ask me: ghostly rappings, levitations, automatic writing, mesmerism…but if a respected man of science endorses the practice, well, maybe there is some credence to it."

"Of course there is nothing to it," I said without opening my eyes. "Continue, Inspector."

"The servants had been sent away for the event and found the awful scene the next morning. Five people were still at the table. Three dead, the so-called spirit medium in some sort of stupor from which we took great pains to arouse him, and his assistant badly injured. The medium calls himself Marcel—we're working on getting his real name—he's about as French as Big Ben—but he put up no resistance to arrest. After subjecting him to close examination, I am happy to say that he confessed to the crime. Justice will be quickly served, I can assure you, as some very prominent people were victims of this fatal chicanery."

I fought to remain calm. "He killed three people and just sat there, waiting to be discovered, until the next day. Did he, perhaps, offer a motive for such unusual criminal behavior?"

"That's the strange part, Mr Holmes. He related that while in a trance, the malevolent spirits he conjured, or channeled within him, somehow caused the fatalities. He took responsibility for opening the door to Death."

"Preposterous," Watson said, spilling some of his tea and attempted to mop up the stain before he could be discovered.

"Hard to believe, I admit," Lestrade shook his head, "yet the servants found the doors and windows to the room locked, there was no sign of violence. All were seated around the table just as casually as we are now."

"Not quite so casually, if they had ceased to be animated," I added. "And what of the assistant?"

"A M. Le Blanc. We were able to revive him; however he was in no condition to give a statement. He was taken to St Bart's."

"A fine picture, Lestrade. A locked room, three dead, the killer willing to confess, no…bear the blame for the action of what… ghosts? Seems like one of your fictional tales, Watson. It is clear that you have not scratched the surface of this case, Lestrade. I fear there is more here, much more."

Lestrade set down his cup. "Well, I did have a few more questions…a few loose ends to tie up. Seeing as you just happen to be in London, Mr Holmes, and, as you have been of assistance to Scotland Yard on one or two occasions—perhaps you would like to accompany me and make some observations…on a purely consulting basis, mind you."

"Consulting. Naturally. There is little time and much to do then. Where are the bodies of the victims being held?"

"At the morgue at St Bart's. Same as Le Blanc."

"Excellent. We shall need to examine the bodies as well as Marcel and LeBlanc, but first we must investigate the crime scene, if it has not already been hopelessly spoiled. Come, Watson. The game is afoot and our quarry has a head start."

Before Mrs Hudson could summon a protest at the state in which we had burst upon and rendered 221B, we were out the door, commandeering Lestrade's driver, and heading from Baker Street through the Paddington Gardens to Marylebone High Street. We soon found ourselves at Spivey House, Westchester. A servant dressed in mourning answered the door and showed us to the parlour where the bodies had been discovered.

I surveyed the room: dark curtains covered the windows, a table with stained velvet surrounded by five chairs. A pen and a bell lay upon the table. "What has been removed from the room, Lestrade?"

Lestrade looked about. "Nothing, except of course, the bodies…oh and the drinks service set upon the side board."

I removed my glass to closely examine the table cloth. "It seems obvious that of the three victims, two were women; both widows, one young, one old. The third person was a military gentleman. They had few close living relations."

"Astounding, Holmes, but how can you have known this from such a cursory evaluation of the premises? We have not released any information as to the identities of the victims."

Watson shot me a knowing glance and stated, "You will find that nothing Sherlock Holmes does is of a cursory nature, Inspector."

"Thank you, dear friend," I said. "You know my methods, Lestrade. We have little time but I am sure that you would have noticed that Spivey House is a venerable old place, yet modern conveniences have been laid on. Note the electric lights and modern furniture and flowers in the foyer: a young woman's touch. However, we sadly note there is not a hint of the masculine upon entering the home. No study off the main hall, no lingering aroma of late night cigars, no trophies. Moreover, one has a clear path to the parlour without avoiding the inevitable accumulation of disarray or toys left in the wake of children. This was a home inherited by a young man who went to war and was lost. The young couple had no time to bear children."

"Lady Penelope Spivey," Lestrade stammered.

"Yet, an ornate sword rests in the umbrella stand in the hall. The black scuff of the boot left upon the floor, admits that a military man was present last evening. The servants could hardly have had time to wipe the mark away. The sword indicates a man of rank, the boot mark shows that his foot drags a bit, the result of some wound to the nerves of the leg, wouldn't you agree, Doctor?" Watson nodded absently. "This must have been one of Spivey's superiors, sent for by his widow to attend the séance. I am speculating here, my knowledge of such things is sparse, but he may have wished to contact either Spivey or other lost comrades through the conveyances of the medium, M. Marcel."

"That would be Colonel Mills," mumbled Lestrade.

"And finally, we come to the hint of perfume in this tightly sealed room. The subtle bouquet is somewhat masked by other odors, but one cannot help recalling a bygone era." I remembered our faithful spaniel, Toby, as the men sniffed about the room in hopes of acquiring the scent. "The aroma is too passé for the lady of the house—hence we detect the presence of an older woman."

Lestrade threw up his hands in resignation. "The Dowager Tsu Ling. Here on a diplomatic errand for the Chinese Consulate."

"Ah, that is why the reluctance to release the names of the victims," Watson observed, still wrinkling his nose above a grey moustache. "To avoid international scandal the police will want to pin down a perpetrator as quickly as possible."

"I fear nothing has been avoided, Doctor. Lestrade, I will beg your leave for a time. Watson and I will venture to the hospital and then rendezvous with you to interview, with your permission, Monsieur Marcel."

"He's not French," Lestrade shook his head and wandered out of the house.

We left Lestrade to rumble off in his motorcar—the offensive thing belching smoke and hemorrhaging noise. I was fortunate to hail one of the few surviving hansom cabs, instructing the driver to avoid the Strand and head north along the river to the hospital.

"What do you make of it, Watson?"

"Hard to say. Lestrade has found a man at the murder scene who has already confessed."

"Convenient for Lestrade, I'd say. Most inconvenient for the accused, if he swings for a murder he didn't commit."

"But surely, sir, you don't give credence to the ranting of char-latans, magicians, and mumbo jumbo men."

"It's not what *we* believe at all, but if the mesmerist and his subjects are convinced of the reality of a phenomenon...." I let the thought trail and we proceeded in silence to our destination.

One would assume that the sight of the dark, rain-soaked in-stitution housing the sick and suffering would promote feelings of melancholy to anyone approaching, but a return to the place where Watson and I first made acquaintance so long ago, did seem a bright ray in the cloud of gloom. We left the cab and made our way through the receiving hall, down back stairs and through a low corridor that wound past my old chemistry laboratory to the morgue. A young attendant sat at a desk reading a newspaper and jotting notes on a pad.

"Help you, gov?" he said without looking up.

"Sherlock Holmes and Dr Watson here to examine the recently murdered."

"Got a lot of bodies, here, man," the clerk said.

"See here!" Watson exclaimed, his grip stiffening on his stick.

"It's all right, Watson. This man suffers a loss and sits confined amongst the dead, wondering if he will ever meet another woman equal to his late wife. We will grant him leeway in his lack of courtesy."

The clerk put down his paper. "How could you know that? What is this?"

"The evidence is clear. I observe you have a mark on your finger where a wedding ring once resided. Your laboratory coat has been poorly pressed—either from neglect or lack of a woman—you are reading the agony column of the paper, searching for a new mate while taking notes, likely preparing to compose your own advertisement. You write this next to the scrawled name *Lestrade* on your house phone log, hence we can assume that the inspector has phoned ahead, and your supervisor, Dr Butlin, alerted you of our imminent visit."

While the baffled attendant attempted to process these revelations, a bearded man in a white smock entered through a side door. "Mr Holmes! Dr Watson! What a surprise, it's been a long time."

"Still at the game?" Watson asked.

"Don't know what else I'd do if I retired. Probably go mad reading books and smoking alone. I could do the same here in better company." Dr Butlin laughed, gesturing to the silent drawers containing the recently departed. "You came to see the bodies." He snapped his fingers and the attendant jumped from his desk and ran to locate the requested victims. Shortly he had the cadavers laid out for our inspection. "Not a mark on them. No sign of violence or struggle."

"Poison, then?" Watson asked.

"It would seem the obvious conclusion, Doctor, yet it would have had to have been an agent with a rapid onset of action to kill three at once. We have analyzed the drinking glasses from the room for arsenic and strychnine but not a trace did we detect. Moreover, those agonizing potions would have left the faces of the deceased in a contortion of pain. Look upon their faces."

"Perfectly calm," I said, "as if in a peaceful slumber."

The doctor continued, "I have tested the stomach contents, naturally, but I detected no unnatural odors on postmortem. In fact, the cause of death eludes me."

"Some sort of death of the mind then?" I mused. "Would you say that these unfortunate people died of fright or in some sort of trance or stupor?"

"It would have to have been a very powerful state induced, to have killed all of the people at once, Mr Holmes. The dowager was elderly, as was the colonel, but he was a man in robust health."

"Military man to the end," Watson said.

"But Mrs Spivey was in the full bloom of youth."

"Broken hearts? Visits from the spirit world?"

"I don't know what to say." Dr Butlin shook his head.

"And yet…this powerful force that brought about the instantaneous death of three also spared both the mesmerist and his assistant. A spiritualist awakens from his trance and finds those about him dead or incapacitated and so naturally assumes that he was somehow the culprit. Tell me what you know of the assistant," I said.

"The man was in bad shape when he came in: stuporous, lividity about the face, quick pulse, which is not unexpected as he was discovered face-down on the table next to the mesmerist. He responded quickly to treatment with brisk massage to the face and extremities and restorative liquors."

"We should waste no time in questioning the fellow," Watson said.

"That will be hard to do," I said. "The man will have left the hospital by now, and as I am sure that he was using an assumed name, will be difficult to track."

Dr Butlin used the telephone to call the hospital ward attendant and confirmed that the patient had fled.

"Scoundrel!" Watson said.

"To be expected," I replied. "Lestrade, complacent in the assumption that he has apprehended his murderer, has let LeBlanc slip away."

"Ghastly! What next, Holmes?" Watson asked.

"We must interview M. Marcel, the only witness to the crime. Watson, be kind enough to telephone your friend, Dr Doyle. He will find this matter of interest and may be of use to us."

Dr Doyle met us at the prison. "A pleasure to see you, gentlemen. I must say that I am unfamiliar of an instance with a séance or mesmeric trance resulting in the deaths of the participants. Most concerning."

"Yet you are convinced of the authenticity of these sessions?" I asked.

"As a man of science, I was initially skeptical but I have witnessed first-hand the power of the spirit realm and the ability of certain persons to channel this energy into an earthly plane. I am certain that the phenomenon is as real as the invisible energy of X-rays or radio waves or the flow of electricity or magnetism."

"Arthur has written extensively on the subject," Watson said.

"Of course, the science will be corrupted by quacks and mountebanks looking to profit from the grief of the bereaved: the nefarious are everywhere. I look forward to assessing the abilities of M. Marcel. I am sure, John, that you have witnessed the power of mesmerism in medical use."

Watson had to admit that he had seen the fakirs of India place themselves in profound states of transfixion. "Yes, and that fellow Dr Eaisdale felt that the mesmeric influence was some sort of animal magnetism that could be transmitted from one person to another. On the other hand, Dr Freud posits that the phenomenon is all in the power of suggestion; he claims that he could place patients into a state of coma such that he could perform amputation of limbs without the sick man sensing any pain whatsoever."

"Regardless of the source, the operator's influence on the mind of the subject must be some force of nature. We must admit to its veracity."

I wasn't convinced.

Lestrade led us to an isolated cell where we met a forlorn Marcel. I attempted in vain to put the man at ease by introducing myself and my colleagues as strict believers in his innocence and of our benevolent intentions to be of assistance.

"I am honored by your attentions, Mr Holmes. But really, I can see no explanation other than that the people who had trusted themselves to my powers, people who had come to me to contact departed loved ones, to ease their suffering, were irrevocably harmed by the process. Mrs Spivey had contacted me in a distraught state after the loss of her husband in the war. His commanding officer, Colonel Mills, friend of the family, had been under a cloud of deep depression due to the loss of so many of his men."

"And what of the Oriental lady?" I inquired.

"Madame Tsu Ling. She was here on a diplomatic mission of some sort. She too had recently lost a loved one, but she was wary and astutely inquired as to how the spirits of dead Chinese could communicate through me in English."

"Yes, that is a bright question," Lestrade added.

"I cannot explain it other than to say that the spirit plane is universal. I assure you that the information that passes through me is almost always confirmed by my subjects as being authentic and containing facts that could only be known to themselves and the departed."

I had no doubt of Marcel's utter sincerity and his beliefs in his gifts, and his motivations to use them for the good. His innate honesty, however, had run him afoul of the law and his confession had placed him in imminent danger of the gallows. "Would you be so kind, Monsieur, and take us through the events of the fateful evening."

Marcel shook his head woefully and seemed to stare vacantly as he recalled the séance. "It won't bring the poor folks back...I am able to place myself in a state receptive to spirit communication. My assistant, M. LeBlanc, is an accomplished mesmerist but remains awake. We have found that by LeBlanc acting as liaison to the sitters, they are guided and made to feel at ease by the experience of contact with the dead. He directs the activities while I am channeling the spirits. That evening, as usual, we sat in a darkened room around a table bare except for a bell to announce the presence of the spirits. Mr LeBlanc had the sitters write the names of the loved ones and any questions that they might wish to ask after I had entered the trance state. In this way, I might add, I can have no foreknowledge of the circumstances of the deaths, or as in the case of Madame Ling, I cannot possibly understand her question as it was written in a language unknown to me. Each sitter affixes their signature to the question and folds the sheet of paper so there can be no tampering."

"You can see, gentlemen," Conan Doyle said, "the use of the scientific method. The medium remains separate from all influences and preconceived notions."

"Lestrade, you no doubt recovered the sheets of paper from the crime scene," I stated.

The inspector seemed ill at ease. "No, Mr Holmes, we did not."

Marcel had begun to perspire. I offered him my kerchief and as he blotted his face I lifted the small lamp that sat on the table and held it above him.

"Doctors, would you witness the markings on M. Marcel's forehead and temples. Note the symmetry of these indentations of the skin." Watson and Doyle leaned in as did Lestrade so that all five of our faces were in close proximity like the weird sisters of *Macbeth*.

"How did you come by these abrasions?" Watson asked.

"I am sure that I do not know," Marcel said, touching his face absently. "Sometimes there are physical manifestations brought about by spirit contact."

"Yes, I have seen emissions of ectoplasm and physical manifestations," said Doyle.

I set the lamp back upon the table. "I think that in this case the markings were made by someone very much alive. Gentlemen, I must inform you that I suspect the sitters of the séance were victims of gas asphyxiation and that M. Marcel is innocent."

"What? Gas!" The four exclaimed nearly in union.

"The conclusion is inescapable. Three dead with no sign of violence or internal poisoning with pleasant expressions upon their faces. Having already been placed in a relaxed state by the mesmeric atmosphere they would have expired peacefully with no obvious outward manifestations."

"Ha! I have you there, Mr Holmes," Lestrade pointed an accusing finger at me. "The Spivey House has all the modern amenities, including electric light! If there was a leak of gas, how is it that Monsieurs Marcel and LeBlanc were unaffected?"

"You will, in fact, find that they *were* affected in some way. Houses converted to electricity still retain intact gas connections. It would be practical for an assailant to restore the flow of gas from the electric chandelier, once a gasolier, into the sealed room. Dr Butlin will confirm that the markings on M. Marcel's face match those of M. LeBlanc. Those pocks upon the skin have been produced by the application of gas masks so widely used in the last war. Once the gas had produced the desired effect, LeBlanc would have opened the vent located high on the wall and concealed by a grill after conversion to electricity. I am sure a search of the ventilation grill will reveal the gas masks stashed inside. LeBlanc would have needed to remain in the room to appear as a victim. Perhaps he intended to open the window to vent more of the gas but he was overcome by lingering fumes. When M. Marcel awoke he was overcome by the ghastly horror to which he thought was provoked by some aspect of his spirit trance gone awry, and as he is a man of most unimpeachable character would have been compelled to confess to a crime to which he had no direct knowledge or involvement." As all present were too astounded to comment,

I continued. "LeBlanc absconded from the hospital, no doubt in possession of the papers containing the signatures of Tsu Ling, Lady Spivey, and Colonel Mills along with personal effects such as keys to homes, safes, and bank boxes. From his haul of items it would have been easy to forge papers of any kind to gain access to a fortune in documents or cash."

"Documents," Lestrade conceded reluctantly. "Madame Ling and Colonel Mills were involved in the tariff negotiations between our government and the Chinese."

"The scoundrel," Doyle said. "Profaning the art of spiritualism for villainous purposes."

"We will have no way to track LeBlanc at this point. He could be halfway across the continent," Watson said.

Doyle thought for a moment and said, "Perhaps there is a way...."

"I must object, Mr Holmes!" Lestrade protested. "This is highly unorthodox."

"Unorthodox situations often beg the use of unorthodox methods, Inspector. Unless you have a viable alternate suggestion as to how to proceed in finding a criminal whom you have allowed to escape, I suggest you let the doctors proceed."

I held the paper out for Lestrade to sign and instructed him to include the name of a deceased loved one. He passed the paper to Doctors Doyle and Watson, who did the same. The lamp was extinguished, plunging the cell into shadow. However, the sounds of rain outside of the barred window and shouts of distraught prisoners echoing through the halls all seemed to recede as M. Marcel began the process of placing his subjects and then himself into a state of mesmerism. I intended to remain awake as vigilant observer to the process.

"We will all now concentrate deeply. Visualize a place of safety, recall times of contentment spent with loved ones who have departed," Marcel began.

"This nonsense will never work on me," were the last words uttered by Lestrade before his face hit the table.

Marcel continued in a commanding, yet soothing voice. "Let all cares escape your mind, you will be relaxed, yearning for peaceful rest, you are safe, you are relaxed, you are in the presence of those you have loved, you are safe..."

The repetition of Marcel's phrases had the desired effect on Watson and Doyle and, as they surrendered to the medium's suggestions, Marcel grew quiet and I saw a new countenance come over him. His contorted facial expression unwound and he seemed to enter into a conversation that at once seemed to be with himself but fractured into different personas.

"Father and Dr Watson, so nice to see you again." Marcel continued in a different voice. "We are in their presence."

"Where are you, son?" Conan Doyle murmured.

"We are so many, we are safe. The war is over?"

"The war is over," Marcel said to himself. "Is your Colonel Mills with you?"

"He is here," Marcel answered himself.

I felt the temperature in the room drop precipitously. Beads of perspiration appeared on Marcel's face. Watson and Doyle seemed to listen intensely with eyes closed and grew restless. Lestrade began to snore.

"Can you help us?" Doyle muttered.

Marcel reached for the pen and papers and began writing furiously. "This is what we know…" As he wrote, his voice changed and became soft with a feminine quality and he recited numbers as I quickly fed him more sheets of paper to keep up with his scribbling. "17, 11, 4, A, 3…20, 12, 9…WHI, 308, 0, 27."

Marcel concluded the séance by writing these three sequences of numbers. Exhausted, he let the pen slip from his hand and slumped backward in his chair. All were asleep and only I had retained my conscious faculties. I went to the door, calling for the jailer, but no one came. I shook Lestrade briskly by the shoulders to rouse him.

"You see, no effect whatsoever," Lestrade said, as if nothing out of the ordinary had occurred. He then noticed the slumbering men at the table. "What is this?"

"There is no time for discussion, Lestrade." I spread the papers across the table.

"Look at this scrawl. Looks to be a bunch of gibberish."

"No, the numbers must have significance. The first sequence of numbers I recognize as account numbers at the Royal Bank. The second sequence would seem to be a combination to a lock."

The close of the banking day was drawing near. By now, LeBlanc would have forged documents containing signatures of

Colonel Mills, Lady Spivey, and Tsu Ling. He would have access to a fortune in money and perhaps secret treaties. Yet even the shifty LeBlanc could not be in several locations at once: he was not at Spivey House, but he would have to act fast to raid the residences of Colonel Mills and Madame Ling and attempt to access the Spivey bank accounts, knowing that once discovered he would need to make a rapid getaway. I beat my fist upon the table rousing Doctors Doyle and Watson and M. Marcel from their comas. "If the first sequence of numbers is the bank account of Lady Spivey then the second must be the combination to Madame Ling's strong box containing the documents. But what is this third sequence? It is too long to be the combination of a lock and too short to be an account number at a bank."

"It's quite elementary, Mr Holmes." Lestrade said. "It's a telephone number."

I cursed my ignorance of the telephone system. I snatched the keys to the cell from Lestrade's belt, opened the door and ran down the hall with the bewildered crowd following. We burst into an office and Lestrade elbowed aside a desk sergeant and handed me the phone. Imagining that shouting would make my voice travel faster to the operator on the line, I bellowed the numbers of the exchange into the contraption.

A woman on the other end answered, her voice oddly sedate, far off, "Royal Bank, Cavendish Square, how may I help you?"

I thrust the receiver into Lestrade's hands. "Dispatch all of your men to Cavendish Square! Have the guards at the bank lock all of the doors. Detain everyone within."

Lestrade, to his credit, sprang into action, barking orders into the telephone and at the sergeant in an efficient, focused manner, devoid of his usual fluster.

"We will hope to have LeBlanc trapped within the bank," I said. Lestrade nodded assent but the woman on the telephone was still speaking. He put the receiver back to his ear and seemed to become perplexed. "The party on the line requests to speak to 'Binky?'"

"That would be me," Watson said, reaching for the phone.

"Well, I hope you had your fun with all this hocus pocus, Dr Doyle. It is perfectly clear that M. Marcel already knew the bank codes and phone number and this…charade…has given ample time for his accomplice to gain a head start on his pursuers," Lestrade said.

Doyle and Marcel began to protest but I raised a hand to silence them. Watson had grown pale, and held the phone limply as a tear glistened on his pallid cheek.

From there I must conclude my account because I have run out of facts. All else is speculation and I leave it to the reader to draw his own conclusions:

LeBlanc was caught red-handed with a draft of the Chinese treaty and the cash from the Spivey account. He was charged with both treason (Lestrade was correct in the assumption that neither Marcel nor LeBlanc were Frenchmen) and murder. Marcel was held as an accomplice for many months, but with only circumstantial evidence against him, he was released. The notoriety from the case only served to enhance his career as a spirit medium. Watson and Doyle would say little more of the experience of the séance at the prison other than to attest that the voice uttered by M. Marcel was that of Doyle's son, Adrien, lost in the war, and that the phone conversation Watson had was with his late wife Mary: beloved, and taken early from this life years before the events described.

—Sherlock Holmes
Sussex Downs, November 1927

HOW WATSON LEARNED THE TRICK

by John H. Watson, M D

In the early 1920's, Queen Mary's Doll's House was built to be exhibited at the British Empire Exhibition. The house was approximately three feet high and was "furnished" with min-iaturized items from Windsor Castle. Several authors were in-vited to write small books to be bound in scaled down volumes; these included works by James M. Barrie, Thomas Hardy, M. R. James, Rudyard Kipling, W. Somerset Maugham, and the following short short piece which shows Watson's good nature in telling this unflattering joke upon himself.

Watson had been watching his companion intently ever since he had sat down to the breakfast table. Holmes happened to look up and catch his eye.

"Well, Watson, what are you thinking about?" he asked.

"About you."

"Me?"

"Yes, Holmes. I was thinking how superficial are these tricks of yours, and how wonderful it is that the public should continue to show interest in them."

"I quite agree," said Holmes. "In fact, I have a recollection that I have myself made a similar remark."

"Your methods," said Watson severely, "are really easily ac-quired."

"No doubt," Holmes answered with a smile. "Perhaps you will yourself give an example of this method of reasoning."

"With pleasure," said Watson. "I am able to say that you were greatly preoccupied when you got up this morning."

"Excellent!" said Holmes. "How could you possibly know that?"

"Because you are usually a very tidy man and yet you have forgotten to shave."

"Dear me! How very clever!" said Holmes. "I had no idea, Watson, that you were so apt a pupil. Has your eagle eye detected anything more?"

"Yes, Holmes. You have a client named Barlow, and you have not been successful with his case."

"Dear me, how could you know that?"

"I saw the name outside his envelope. When you opened it you gave a groan and thrust it into your pocket with a frown on your face."

"Admirable! You are indeed observant. Any other points?"

"I fear, Holmes, that you have taken to financial speculation."

"How *could* you tell that, Watson?"

"You opened the paper, turned to the financial page, and gave a loud exclamation of interest."

"Well, that is very clever of you, Watson. Any more?"

"Yes, Holmes, you have put on your black coat, instead of your dressing gown, which proves that your are expecting some important visitor at once."

"Anything more?"

"I have no doubt that I could find other points, Holmes, but I only give you these few, in order to show you that there are other people in the world who can be as clever as you."

"And some not so clever," said Holmes. "I admit that they are few, but I am afraid, my dear Watson, that I must count you among them."

"What do you mean, Holmes?"

"Well, my dear fellow, I fear your deductions have not been so happy as I should have wished."

"You mean that I was mistaken."

"Just a little that way, I fear. Let us take the points in their order: I did not shave because I have sent my razor to be sharpened. I put on my coat because I have, worse luck, an early meeting with my dentist. His name is Barlow, and the letter was to confirm the appointment. The cricket page is beside the financial one, and I turned to it to find if Surrey was holding its own against Kent. But go on, Watson, go on! It's a very superficial trick, and no doubt you will soon acquire it."

✗

www.ingramcontent.com/pod-product-compliance
Lightning Source LLC
Chambersburg PA
CBHW051832170626
46807CB00003B/1147